JUNGLE RESCUE

Also by Timothy Peters

The Josh Powers Series:
Desert Rescue
Alaskan Rescue
Rescue From Camp Wildwood
The Rescue of Josh Powers

JUNGLE RESCUE

TIMOTHY PETERS

ABUNDANT HARVEST
PUBLISHING

Jungle Rescue
Copyright © 2019 by Timothy Peters

ALL RIGHTS RESERVED
No portion of this book may be reproduced, stored in any
retrieval system, or transmitted in any form or by any
means, electronic, mechanical, photocopy, recording or
otherwise, without the express written consent of the
author.

Formatting: Erik V. Sahakian
Cover Design/Layout/Photo: Andrew Enos

All Scripture is taken from the New King James Version of
the Bible. Copyright © 1979, 1980, 1982 by Thomas
Nelson, Inc. Used by permission. All rights reserved.

Library of Congress Control Number: 2019937788

ISBN 978-1-7327173-4-3
Second Printing: September 2019

FOR INFORMATION CONTACT:

Abundant Harvest Publishing
35145 Oak Glen Rd
Yucaipa, CA 92399
www.abundantharvestpublishing.com

Printed in the United States of America

TABLE OF CONTENTS

To my loving wife, Shawn, for giving me all the time I needed to write.

Jeremiah Peters: missionary, pilot, and airframe and power-plant mechanic, for technical support.

Erik Sahakian for reading and formatting.

Andrew Enos for graphic design.

Thank you all.

Prologue

Josh' father, Doug Powers, had been kidnapped. A local drug dealer, in the jungles of El Salvador, had turned Doug Powers' life into a nightmare. Though Josh' parents were missionaries here for many years, this notorious drug dealer believed that Powers was spying for the Drug Enforcement Agency.

When Josh was two years old his dad had started Gospel Air Transportation Enterprises.

Doug Powers hacked the runway out of the jungle with a chainsaw and shovel. The family then moved to the remote airstrip because he said it was in the middle of missionary country.

For six months now Doug Powers waited to be rescued. Josh' mother had no idea where her husband was. After his disappearance, she returned to the United States to get help. No one seemed to be able— or willing—to do anything. Just when she was about to give up hope, she received a puzzling phone call in the middle of the night.

"Do you have a son who can fly an airplane?" said a man with a heavy accent.

"Who is this?" Josh' mother asked.

"Your husband says he is only in this country to help my people. But he must prove to us that he is not a DEA agent. If you have a young son who can fly a plane, as your husband has said, we will believe what he has told us. Have your son pick your husband up at the airstrip near Malo Falls. He must come alone."

Click.

The phone woke Josh up. He walked to his mother's room. "Who was that?"

His mother had a puzzled look on her face. "I don't know. The man said he's holding your dad and he wants you to go to El Salvador and pick him up. He wants you to fly into our compound and get him. Joshua, I don't like this." Tears streamed down her face. "Someone else should go. You're too young. It's too risky."

But the next morning, his mother shuffled into the kitchen where Josh was eating breakfast; her hair ruffled and her eyes were bloodshot. "Joshua ... Joshua, I struggled and prayed about this the rest of the night. And God has given me peace about you going to El Salvador. We'll book you a flight on Central Airlines. Upon your arrival, find your dad's airplane and fly to the com-pound."

Josh was petrified. But he was more afraid of what might happen to his dad if he didn't go. He left the next day but soon found out that even the best of plans can quickly go wrong.

Chapter 1

Black, smelly smoke convinced fourteen-year-old Joshua Powers he was in real trouble. Seconds before, there was a loud slapping sound on the side of the airplane. It sounded like someone hit it with a hammer. He was cruising high above the dark green jungle of El Salvador in his father's Cessna 150—the same plane in which Doug Powers had taught him how to fly.

The noise terrified him and the thick smoke filling the cockpit told him he would have to crash-land. He spotted the waterfall near the small dirt airstrip which had been his home for most of his life.

Josh' blue eyes flashed across the instrument panel. His heart raced when he saw the oil pressure gauge slowly moving toward zero. At any second the engine would seize and plunge him to the earth far short of the runway.

The hot, black oil crept across the windshield like lava from a volcano; he choked from the smoke and heat rising in the cockpit. Gradually, the oil covered the front window and oozed around to the side windows, cutting off his vision. His hand flew to the latch on the window. The three-inch gap at the bottom sucked the smoke out, but it didn't help him see.

Slamming his left elbow into the old, yellowed Plexiglas® several times, Josh forced an opening large enough to stick his head through. He had a sickening feeling in the pit of his stomach when he saw the trees below. The engine was slowly grinding to a halt, and the plane was losing altitude fast.

Taking his blue baseball cap off, he stuck his face out of the hole in the window. His eyes searched the jungle looking for a safe place to land. Then the engine froze. The propeller stopped turning and all he could hear was the rushing of the wind. He couldn't see any clearing in the forest. His next thought was the trees, but the trees would shred the plane and kill him. The river was his only chance. He hoped it wasn't too deep.

"Well, the river it is then." Josh clenched his teeth and brushed strands of light brown hair out of his face. Then his hands automatically went through all the motions his father had trained him to do. With his left hand, Josh held the control wheel, while his right hand flitted to the fuel selectors and turned them off. From there he reached down between the seats and pulled up gently on the flap control lever. The flaps slowed the plane and gave the wings more lift.

The shrill whine of the stall-warning horn sent shivers through his already tense body. He tried to hold

12

the airplane steady by pulling back on the control wheel. Josh hadn't realized he was doing this until that unmistakable noise. It would be a fatal mistake if he did not relax and let the airplane carry enough speed to fly.

Glancing out of the hole in the window, he realized he would have to turn or miss the river completely. His left foot stabbed down on the rudder pedal as his hand managed the control wheel. The plane flashed by the face of the waterfall and Josh felt it slow as it turned into the breeze blowing upriver. He rolled the airplane back to level flight and pointed it toward the river.

"I don't know if this bush pilot can do this!" About the time he got those words out of his mouth he re-membered why he was there. "Dad!" he shouted.

His mind whirled with thoughts of his father, which were suddenly interrupted by the tops of the trees flying past his window. Maybe his dad had seen the trailing black smoke of the airplane when it turned away from the falls, heading downriver to crash.

Josh stuck his head out of the hole to make sure he was lined up with the river. Hot, dirty, black oil splattered on his face. The muddy brown river seemed to reach up with grimy hands to snatch the small plane from the sky. His left hand reached for the master switch and flipped it to the off position.

Could he do this? Josh never actually had to do an emergency landing. He had practiced with his dad, but they would only go down to one hundred feet. This time he had to go all the way down, and land in a river. Not a nice safe field, but a river.

With both hands, Josh pulled back gently on the control wheel. His feet played the rudder pedals to keep the airplane straight. The plane slowed and he released some of the pressure on the wheel. Suddenly, he remembered one important procedure—a Mayday call. He pushed the microphone bottom on the control wheel and yelled.

"Mayday, Mayday, Mayday!"

Then Josh turned his attention back to landing the plane. He continued to slow the airplane, but a giant tree struck the right wing. The plane moaned as the wing was wrenched off the fuselage. Twisting to the right, the airplane slid sideways through the air, it bounced, then slammed into the rusty brown water.

"Oh God help me!"

The airplane was dragged down river, twisting and turning, and crashing on jagged rocks. The roar of the raging river and the moan of the metal in the water was deafening. He thought the thrashing would never stop. Finally, the small plane came to rest in the gravel on the bottom of the river.

Water and gas poured through the broken window. The cockpit was filling fast, and his hands flew up looking for his seatbelt latch. He had unhooked the seatbelt a hundred times, but in his panic to get out, he couldn't find the buckle. He realized his body had twisted during the crash, and calmed himself enough to trace the belt around to the buckle. Just as the water covered his nose, his fingers set him free.

As the water rose, he hardly had time to take a breath. He reached for the handle on the passenger's side and tried to open the door. To his horror, it was locked. In the few seconds it took to unlock the door, the cockpit filled with water. Josh thrashed and kicked to get out.

"Jesus save me!" As he fumbled around inside the small water-filled space he realized his face was out of the water.

A small pocket of air was trapped in one corner of the cockpit. Drawing a deep breath into his aching lungs helped him enough to think. He was sure the plane was underwater, but how far? Was it two feet or twenty feet? Could he make it to the surface?

The water smelled and tasted like aviation gas. The mixture of mud and gas burned his eyes. He fumbled around to find the door handle. Putting his feet on the door of the plane, he took several large gulps of air, turned the handle and pushed up with all his might. The lightweight aluminum door flew open.

The airplane had settled in just enough water to cover it. Relieved, Josh climbed out of the plane, choking and coughing from the smell and taste of high-octane gasoline. The water had a beautiful, but deadly, rainbow of gasoline and oil floating on the surface and streaming off. If any spark was left glowing, the gas could flash and burn him, and the remains of the small plane.

He caught one of his pant legs on the sharp jagged edge of the wreckage and tumbled headfirst into the river. When he pulled himself up, he noticed his baseball cap floating inside the cockpit.

"Never go into the jungle without a hat." It was one of his family's silly rules. His father would say it to anyone who got within a hundred feet of the jungle.

Josh grabbed his soggy hat and swam through the water. *Only a few feet left to go.* He was exhausted when he crawled onto the bank. His clothes were torn and soaking wet; his boots were filled with mud which felt like weights inside of them. He stumbled onto the warm ground.

The sun felt good on his cheeks as he lay there, glad to be alive. He thought about his dad. *He's probably waiting on the airstrip, wondering where his son is.* Josh groaned. *Why did I cry out to God before the crash? I never cry out to God.*

He had lived most of his young life on his father's faith. His father trusted God completely. Everything good was God's work and everything bad just gave him another reason to trust God for the outcome. Josh didn't know if he believed that or not.

When he was twelve years old he went to the United States to live with family friends. He attended school, and left his "little boy" faith in the jungle with his parents. Since he was away from them, he decided he would be his own person, and make his own decision on what he believed.

But something had gone wrong. In the middle of the crash, he called out to the Lord. He never thought much of people who only wanted God around when they were in trouble, but that's what he had done.

Josh wondered if God saved him or was it dumb luck. He had seen crashes with less damage to the airplane and killed the pilot. But right now, he really didn't want to deal with any of that. He had to think about getting himself to the top of the falls and into the compound where his father was held.

Even though Josh was lying in direct sunlight, he was shivering, and sore. Though nothing felt broken, something didn't feel quite right. He tried to remember what he had learned in that boring First Aid class in school. *Keep the patient warm.* That was the only thing he remembered the teacher saying, but he couldn't remember why. Then ... *Shock. That's it, shock. Shock was the reason to keep the patient warm.*

When he tried to get to his feet, he discovered that his whole body ached. Between the shaking and the pain, he could only make it to the edge of the dark green tree line. There he collapsed onto the musty, thick pile of leaves covering the ground.

By moving his arms as if he were swimming, Josh scraped out a trench. He slithered into the trench and rolled onto his back. His hands shook violently as he tried to zip his soaking wet leather jacket. After several tries, the zipper worked and he scooped giant leaves over his body. The leaves were like a blanket trapping his body heat; warmth of the leaves, and even the soreness of his body, made it easier for Josh to fall asleep.

But minutes later the sound of the rain on the leaves woke him. In his effort to keep warm, he had covered his face with a leaf the size of his chest. When he pulled it away, he was startled by the darkness. For a second, he wondered if he had gone blind until he caught the faint glimmer of light glowing on his wristwatch.

Pulling the gigantic leaf umbrella back over his face, Josh tried to relax. That's when he realized his legs were numb and cold. Cooler than the rest of his body. He worried that he might have injured his back.

His hands threw off leaves like a dog digging for bones. When he got down to his pants, he noticed his legs were underwater. The rain had caused the muddy river to swell and water began to fill his life-saving trench. He needed to move to higher ground fast, but didn't know which way to go. He knew where the jungle was from the river, but wasn't sure if he could get far enough or high enough, away from the raging water. The thick darkness made it impossible to see. He felt alone. His eyes strained to see the illuminated face of his watch.

"Never go into the jungle without matches," was what his dad always told him. It was another of his

18

father's sayings he had joked about. But as Josh unzipped his jacket and reached for the matches in an inside pocket, he was glad he had listened to his father.

Doug Powers insisted they carry a waterproof container of matches and a separate container with cotton balls smeared in petroleum jelly. When you lit the cotton ball, it burned hot and long, drying out wet wood even in a rainstorm.

Josh crept away from the noise of the river. Every time his hands touched a small wooden stick, he picked it up and stuffed it inside his jacket. He crawled until the jungle canopy sheltered him from most of the rain. Groping around in the darkness, he finally located a large tree and sat with his back resting against it.

He found a large green leaf off a banana tree, and folded one end down behind his head, draping the other end across his knees. Under the leaf umbrella, he took the small wet sticks from his jacket and stacked them on the ground like a teepee. Then he reached for the two metal vials inside his jacket. If he dropped either one of them, it would be impossible to find in the dark. And with all the leaves and sticks on the ground, he might not even find them in the daylight.

Carefully, he pulled out one of the containers and gently unscrewed the lid. With his index finger he could feel the greasy cotton balls. His finger raked the ball up the inside of the container into the palm of his hand. His fingers trembled as they squeezed their precious cargo. He would not have held a diamond tighter than he did that little cotton ball.

After sliding the container back into his pocket, Josh pulled out the brass case containing the matches. He unscrewed the lid, took out a match, clinching it between his teeth.

Reaching down under the leafy umbrella, Josh found the stick teepee. With one hand he slipped the cotton ball under the sticks and kept his hand on the wood. With his other hand he took the match from his teeth. Josh placed the large end of the match against the zipper on his jacket. "Well, here goes." With a quick motion, he struck the match along the brass.

A tiny piece of the match head broke off, flared, and shot away like a tiny shooting star. His shaking hand placed the head of the match on the zipper for a second try.

On the second strike, the match popped and flared to life. The flash was so bright, it created a blue spot in the center of his vision. He tried to look around the spot as he moved the flame toward the cotton ball.

The tiny ball of cotton, smoked and smoldered too long and Josh feared it would not light. After what seemed like forever, the cotton ball burst into flames. He cautiously laid the remaining piece of matchstick on the flame and started to feed the smallest sticks into the tiny fire. As they dried and caught fire, he slipped larger sticks into the flames. He continued this until he thought the fire would burn on its own.

When he finally looked up, his little fire had pushed back the darkness and held it inside a large ring around him. The circle of light was his whole world.

For the first time in hours, Josh forced himself to stand. His body, bruised and scraped, still ached. But he had to gather more wood within his small, lighted world before his fire went out.

When he had done all he could, he had nothing left but to think and wait. Again he wondered about his father waiting at the top of the falls and wished desperately he could be there. The warmth of the fire soothed him but the rain brought different smells. It seemed to be a mixture of sweet fragrance and rot.

Several plants blended their scent with the rain, trying to cover the ever-present odor of decaying leaves. His father wanted him to be thankful for everything, even the smell of the jungle. Josh thought his dad was strange to give thanks for the smell of rot. Yet Doug Powers seemed truly thankful and also believed that God was in control. Josh remembered his cry for help and surviving the crash. *Maybe Dad is right.*

The rain fell harder. He threw more sticks onto the fire and snuggled back against the tree trunk, closing his eyes and folding his hands. "God, I haven't done this in a long time. I don't even know if you hear me. But if you do, I need your help. Thank you for helping me today. Oh, and thank you for being with my dad. Amen."

Josh stared into the glowing red embers of the fire. He didn't like the dark. It felt like someone, or something, was watching him. He couldn't wait for the long, lonely night to be over.

Chapter 2

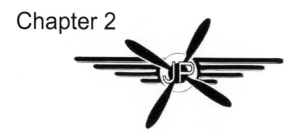

The hot, bright sun, and the musty smell woke Josh to a new day. The storm that had swollen the river to an angry flood had passed; its dark clouds drifting away. The fire, his companion for most of the night, smoldered in tiny gray ringlets of smoke ascending into the still morning air. The only sound Josh could hear was the roar of the river.

His mouth was as dry as the desert, and besides the aches and pains from the crash, his stomach growled from hunger. His father kept the airplanes stocked with a survival kit. Now all he had to do was find it.

Using the lower branches of a tree he pulled himself up and walked toward the river's edge, where he hoped to find the survival kit, and food. The plane was in three feet of water the day before. Would he still be able to find it?

Pushing his way through the underbrush, Josh was surprised to find the river only twenty feet from his camp. The river was wild and had cut a new path through the jungle. But there was no trace of the little blue and white airplane.

He shoved his way around some brush to see up the river in hopes he had just looked the wrong way. But there wasn't a sign of the broken airplane, except part of the wing which swung high from a branch.

Josh found his way back to the campsite and threw some firewood on the glowing coals. He blew the fire back to life and started to plan things out.

He figured he was two miles from the base of the falls. It took the airplane only a few seconds to hit the water after he turned downstream. If he followed the river he should be able to reach the falls in a couple of hours, and then get to the top of the falls and into his father's compound. Although the river was running well above the tree line, he thought it might take longer to force his way through the underbrush.

He scooped up several armloads of wet mulch and tossed it onto his fire. The wet leaves turned the flames into a cloud of smoke and steam. Then, not twenty feet from his camp, he spotted footprints in the mud—panther footprints. The big cat must have paced nearby, but never got too close. "There really was something watching me last night." *The fire might have frightened if off.* Josh blew out a sigh of relief.

Looking around and over his shoulder, to make sure the panther was gone, he started out for the falls.

With the river swollen the hike was more difficult. And the muddy water forced him to walk far back into the shadows of the trees. The floor of the jungle was littered with fallen branches. And a snarl of vines grew over, under, and around everything. It took most of his strength to push through the waist high tangle.

Many grunts and deep breaths later Josh moved back to the water's edge to check his progress. His lean body bent over; hands on knees. But when he looked upstream, the piece of the wing which was stuck in a tree only seemed as far away as it was when he first started out. He checked his watch. For an hour now, Josh had fought his way through the jungle. And looking down the river, not two hundred yards from where he stood was the thin pillar of smoke rising from his dying campfire. He kicked the brush and groaned.

The heat from the blazing sun beat down on his head. He took his cap off and wiped his face and head with his red bandanna. Peeling off his smelly, wet flight jacket, he wrapped it around his waist by the sleeves.

He forced himself to move forward, though he was tempted to just sit and wait—for what, he didn't know.

The roar of an airplane overhead drowned out his thoughts and the sound of rushing water. He looked up and saw the familiar shape of an old twin engine Beech 18. There on the bottom of the wings in big, bold black letters was written, "Cristo te ama": Jesus loves you in Spanish. It was his dad's airplane and Josh was surprised at how bad it looked.

25

The Beech 18 was his dad's favorite plane. A doctor had given the plane to GATE because he had no use for it anymore. It was too slow and used too much gas, but Josh' dad loved it. It was the perfect airplane to land on the dirt runway. Josh jumped to his feet and waited for the airplane to circle around. Quickly, he pulled his jacket off his waist, ready to wave. But the airplane continued downriver.

Josh jumped up and down, waving his arms. "Here! Down here!"

The skin of the plane was tarnished and black. Dirty oil trailed under the wings behind both engines. His dad had always kept it spotless so Josh assumed someone else had been using it.

For a while he stood frozen until the plane disappeared. Then he turned, and once again set off for the waterfall. He was angry as he plowed into the tangle like a bulldozer. *Why is it up to me to rescue Dad?*

But after fifteen minutes, his strength began to fail. Josh leaned against a fallen tree. *I better use my head instead of muscle.* So he picked the easier route which made his going slower, but at least he was making progress. He kept going even when the tangled vines ripped his shirt and scratched his skin.

Slowly Josh worked his way back to the river where he plopped down in the soft sand to catch his breath. The churning, rust-colored water had receded, but was still well above its banks.

Using a stick, he cut a trench away from the water's edge. A little trickle of water followed the stick. With his hand he gouged out a small pool for the water. If he waited a few minutes the sand and mud would sink to the bottom of his little pool and leave cool, clear water for him to drink.

When the pool was full, Josh cut off the flow into his trench. He sat back on his elbows to wait for the water to clear. All the while his head throbbed from the lack of water and his stomach rumbled.

When the water cleared, Josh couldn't wait any longer. He laid his bandana across the surface of the water and sucked up the precious liquid of life-saving coolness. It eased the ache in his stomach.

As Josh turned onto his back, out of the corner of his eye he caught a glimpse of something bright yellow. The color stood out from the jungle's many shades of green. No more than twenty feet from where he lay in the sand, was the most feared animal in the jungle: a giant black panther. The people called it *El Espiritu Negro*—the Black Spirit.

The panther slowly sank to attack position. Its big yellow eyes narrowed and its tail swished back and forth. In a split second, the cat could be on him.

Josh rolled into the muddy water just as the panther started to leap. Fear choked Josh' throat like a noose, but as the water drug him downstream, he watched the cat race off into the jungle.

Mud filled his clothes, and he sank like a rock. His body twisted, and spun, bounced off the bottom, then shot into the air. The whole process repeated itself more than once. Josh struggled to keep his head above water so he could breathe. With one hand he held the knot that tied the sleeves of his jacket around his waist, and with the other he swam. But the current dragged him under.

His stomach filled with rusty water and his lungs gasped for air. When he thought he would have to suck in more of the muddy water, his head would break out. In those seconds of freedom, he tried to gulp as much air as he could before slamming to the bottom again.

It was like falling through a black hole. He couldn't even tell which way was up.

"God, help me! I want to live!"

All of a sudden he reached the surface and spotted the nearby shore. He tried to paddle toward the bank, but the water had him upside down. Suddenly, to his relief, the water changed to a fast, but smooth river. This gave him a chance to get his head above water for a few seconds. The river curved to the left and swept him toward the right bank.

Halfway around the curve a large tree floated in the water. His only chance was to get washed into the branches. He fumbled with the sleeves of his jacket to make the knot tighter. The leather did not want to move. He realized he could drown so he let go of the sleeves and swam as hard as he could in this torrent.

The current smashed him into the branches. He grabbed the limbs and held on with one hand; struggling to free his other from a tangle below the water. When he finally got both hands around one large branch, he didn't have enough strength to pull himself up.

Luckily, the water rushing passed his legs washed the silt out of his pants. His legs got lighter and floated to the surface. Josh hung from the branch and finally made his way toward the bank. Hand over hand he dragged himself along each branch until he could put his feet on a limb just below the surface of the water.

As he stood on his tired legs, the tree shuddered and moved by the force of the river. Josh scrambled for the bank. The closer he got to the sandy bank the faster the tree moved. With one final leap, he jumped for the shore just as the tree got pulled into the river and was carried off downstream. He landed on his hands and knees in a few inches of water and scampered for dry ground. There he threw up the muddy water. His hands shook uncontrollably as he covered it with dirt. He cleaned his face, and rolled over onto his back on the warm sand. His blue baseball cap was gone, but at least he still had his matches.

Josh slept through most of that day. When he woke, the sun was low in the western sky. He believed he could still make a little headway toward Malo Falls.

The river had gone down and was a wide path of sand, rocks and broken tree limbs. This time he decided to stay out of the trees and walk through the rubble near the river's edge. He grimaced with every step. And as he rounded a corner in the river, he spotted the smoke from his morning fire lazily drifting skyward. Josh hung his head. He realized he had spent the whole day trying to get to his father's compound, but only ended up back at his starting point.

He stumbled to the pile of smoldering leaves and uncovered the charred wood. The larger pieces were still red hot. With a few dry twigs and leaves, Josh was able to prod his fire back to life for the third time. He gathered all the firewood he could.

As the darkness and night noises set in, Josh dug a new sleeping trench and filled the bottom with fresh, dry leaves. He silently cursed the Black Panther. *Crazy panther, brought me right back to where I started.* He piled the fire with twigs and leaves before settling into his bed for another lonely night.

As he lay staring upriver, he noticed a faint glow of light at the top of the hill above the falls. The small orange light changed into a great white arch. A full moon slowly lifted into the night sky. Josh was two miles from the compound, and from his father. With the moonlight and a crackling fire, he knew he could make it alone in the jungle one more night.

Chapter 3

Bug bites on his arms and face reminded Josh he was still in the jungle. Black-Fly bites covered his hands. He counted twelve bites in a one square inch and stopped counting.

When he stretched, his entire body hurt. He would have stayed in his jungle bed longer, but he was bothered by stomach cramps. He tried to remember what his friend Tolando had said about what, and where in the jungle he could find things to eat, but his starved body only wanted a Big Mac.

Josh laughed when he remembered the giant grubs Tolando had dug out of a fallen tree. They were as big as his thumb and pale yellow. Tolando had lit a fire by striking two stones together. From a gigantic leaf he made a bowl and the liquid that oozed out of the leaf kept
it from burning while he roasted the grubs.

When the pale yellow color turned to dark brown, Tolando popped one of the grubs into his mouth and offered the other one to Josh. When he worked up the nerve to try it, Josh was surprised by its cheesy taste. From that time on, Josh tried everything Tolando offered him to eat.

But thinking of food, even grubs, made his hunger worse. The only thing he could do now for a good meal was to reach the compound. He crawled out of his bed.

Surprisingly, the river was back to normal size. The edge, where the water had cleared the forest, was littered with broken trees and boulders. Josh decided to follow the river and stay out of the trees. He turned around, scooped an armload of leaves and tossed them on the fire. The steam hissed as it rose to the top of the trees.

Above the treetops, Josh heard the roar and whistle of his dad's old plane. He watched it fly down the river and turn the same direction it had the day before. This time he didn't try to get their attention.

Then, as he turned and started for the river, he froze with fear. Not fifteen feet away was an Alasa spear stabbed into the ground. The bright red tail feather of a Macaw flapped in the breeze like a small flag. Tolando had warned Josh that to pass a spear with a red feather was death.

Tolando was the only Alasa Indian he had ever seen. He showed up at their airstrip one day. They looked like they were about the same age, but it was impossible to tell. They couldn't understand each other, even though the two boys played together like old friends.

Josh thought of him as he quietly slipped behind a large boulder and pressed himself into the wet ground. For several minutes, he lay hidden behind the boulder wondering what to do next.

Slowly, he got up on his hands and knees and peeked around the rock. On the ground near the spear, he noticed something familiar. The Alasa had a certain way of folding leaves to make bowls. All their food was served that way. Near the shaft was one of these bowls full of steaming, hot food. Josh was puzzled. He knew that the spear was a warning sign, but why the food?

He scanned the tree line, curious to see if he would catch a glimpse of the Indian who had left the warning spear and food. Josh was amazed that someone could come so close and not be seen or heard.

In the Indian dialect Alasa meant, The Unseen Ones. And they didn't want to be seen, as outsiders were always trying to do them harm. The Alasa had killed some loggers who were burning the rain forest. The men who survived the attack said their attackers were unseen. From that time on, the whole tribe was fair game.

And though Josh knew he might not ever see the Indian who left the bowl of food, he searched for him anyway—deciding if the person had wanted to kill him, he would already be dead. The question remained: Did the Alasa want him to have the food or was it a warning?

His stomach made the final decision. Carefully, he turned and crawled as low to the ground as he could; stopping now and then to look around. He grabbed the bowl and went back to the rock.

The first bite was a handful of wild rice that he stuffed into his mouth. Secret flavors of the Alasa food caused him to moan with delight. After the first mouthful, he slowed down and enjoyed every bite. Everything in the bowl was something Tolando had given him to eat in the past. Could Tolando have left the food?

Again Josh felt like he was being watched. It made him nervous. With his breakfast out of the way, Josh set out for the compound. But he hesitated, as if he had forgotten something, and walked back to the spear for one last look. On the ground next to the brightly colored shaft was a small circle of stones. Inside the circle was a line of stones pointing the way he should go. Tolando had taught Josh that sign on their many adventures into the jungle.

Tolando had come every day to be with Josh, but he would never talk to an adult or go inside a house. At first, Doug Powers was worried that Tolando would take Josh into the forest and never bring him back. But as time passed Josh' dad began to trust Tolando.

At first he let the two boys go into the jungle on short trips. The trips became longer and soon they were out overnight. Tolando revealed many of the Alasa's secrets of the forest. His dad was convinced that this contact with the Alasa was what God had planned.

Josh looked at the small circle of stones which were used to give directions to one another. Each stone was so tiny that an untrained eye wouldn't notice the sign. The only problem was they were pointing toward the jungle. This disturbed Josh. *Why does he want me to go into the jungle?* He decided to follow the river instead.

With shoulders stooped over, Josh walked along the riverbank for quarter of a mile. In a clearing by some fallen trees, he spotted yet another spear and a circle of stones. This time the stones were larger and more defined. The Indian who made this marker didn't want Josh to miss it. He stopped and searched the dark green tree line for any sign of whoever left the marker. Josh wanted to yell for Tolando, but he knew an Alasa would never answer.

He ignored the sign and continued up the river. The fallen trees and upturned rocks became harder and harder to cross. Every now and then, Josh came to another marker. Each marker was bigger than the last and pointed into the forest.

Josh continued on the river's edge until he came to a pile of flood rubble too large to get around. Jammed between the standing trees, on each side of the river, was a mound of branches, tree trunks, and brush that formed a dam twenty feet high.

On the ground at the base of the dam, was a giant Alasa direction marker and a warning spear with two bright red feathers. He couldn't climb over the rubble and he didn't want to try and cross the river again. The only thing Josh could do, was follow the markers.

God, am I doing the right thing?

The path reminded Josh of the days when he followed Tolando through the jungle. His Indian friend would point out the trails marked by an unseen person.

Josh checked the direction with his watch. His father had taught him to use his wristwatch like a compass. If he pointed the hour hand at the sun, halfway between the twelve and the hour hand was south. From this reference point, Josh could keep track of the direction he traveled.

He was careful to count the steps from one marker to the next. The Alasa put a marker every seventy-five paces unless they needed to change direction. When he found the next marker, he turned that direction, checked his watch, and headed off to the next one. The path he followed took him deeper into the forest. It bothered him that it wasn't taking him in the direction he wanted to go. But he decided to stick to this path a little longer.

The steps to the next marker led him through a small opening in the bottom of a tangled vine. Directly in front of him was a well-worn, hard packed dirt trail.

He had never seen anything like it in all his travels in the jungle.

Ducking back into the vine tunnel, he quickly checked his watch for the direction and discovered that this jungle highway headed straight toward the compound. Josh jumped to his feet. With both hands he brushed the dirt and leaves off his clothes and started up the trail toward the compound.

He walked as fast as his sore body would let him. It was hard for him to breathe with this jungle heat and humidity. And his brown leather jacket felt like a steam bath inside. But soon Josh could hear the sound of the river as the trail turned back toward the water.

As he rounded the bend in the path, a bright red feather twisted gently on a leather strip, tied to the end of an Alasa spear. The colorful lance was jammed right in the center of the trail. Near the point of the spear was the only direction marker he had seen since he started on the well-worn trail. The marker pointed back toward the river. Josh grabbed the spear, jumped off the trail, and took cover under a large bush.

"I don't get it," he mumbled. "I thought he wanted me to follow the trail into the forest." The Alasa could find their way through the thickest jungle on the darkest night. They wouldn't make a mistake of marking the wrong direction in daylight. Why didn't they want him to follow the trail now?

The silence of the jungle caught his attention. No birds chirped and no monkeys screeched.

Everything was quiet except for the whispering of the trees and distant babble of water.

Josh stretched out flat on the ground and covered his body with leaves as quietly as he could. He held his breath, straining to hear what had caused the silence. The longer he waited the tenser he grew. He wanted this nightmare over and thought of running toward the compound.

But then, through the trees, he heard a murmur. His body stiffened and he started to sweat. His breath was so shallow he feared he would pass out.

The murmur, now the faint sound of people singing, seemed to be heading in the same direction he was. As they got closer, he wanted to jump up and yell. He wanted to walk to his father's compound with them, but something told him to watch and wait.

Josh slithered to a spot where he could get a better look, but not be seen. He ran his hands through the dirt and put diagonal stripes on his face so he would blend in with the shrubs.

Within a few seconds the leader of the group came into view. He looked like one of the local men, but in place of their customary machete was an AK-47. And he was the only one not singing. Twenty feet behind him came the line of singing men and women. Many of them carried guns and had large, burlap bundles tied on their backs.

Josh waited until the last person passed before he took a breath. Then, slowly he got to his feet watching the procession move up the trail. He was about to follow them when he heard something and saw movement out of the corner of his eye. Without thinking, he dove back to his hiding place.

There was a crouched man on the trail behind him. The man crawled toward him with his weapon ready. Josh moved a little to the right. He could feel his heart pounding against the ground. Sweat was running down his face into his mouth.

The man was close; Josh could see his face. He was shocked to see it was not a man at all. The gunman was a girl about his age. She was as scared as he was and perhaps searching for whatever had made that sound he had just heard. If he even blinked, she would find him. He held his breath.

When they were about ten feet apart, the clatter of gunfire echoed through the jungle. Someone up the trail was shooting. The girl jumped to her feet and in a panic fired her weapon just over Josh's head and ran up the trail.

His mouth felt full of cotton and he almost threw up again. But he lay still, in the same spot, in the same position, for over an hour. Finally, he sat up and wiped his face clean.

The warning spears took on new meaning. The Alasa must have known where the real danger was. Something was definitely wrong. Josh knew he had better be more cautious. He decided he needed to follow the direction of the trail, but stay back in the shadows of the trees.

For the first time, Josh realized his father's kidnapping was not just a matter of mistaken identity. These people were dangerous. He moved as fast and as quietly as he could, listening for any sound of danger.

He was so focused on the task at hand that he almost missed the thunderous sound of the water going over the falls. He was near Malo Falls, away from the trail. From here on he would follow the river.

Cautiously, he walked in the dark shadows, travelling in quick short trips from tree to tree. Near the bottom of the falls, he crawled to the rocks at the water's edge.

He moved his head slowly around the side of the boulder until he could see the water. The pond, the family's swimming hole, was now a dump. The once clear, cool water was now a muddy mess from the flood, and debris slowed the flow of water.

As Josh looked about this terrible scene, he recognized a few of his family's belongings in the water: furniture, clothing, toys, and even the old fuel barrels had been pushed over the falls.

On the far side of the pond was a little cardboard hut with a palm-frown roof. A fire burned in front of the door and a dented, burnt black pan sat on a rock. Josh pulled back as soon as he saw movement inside the hut.

A twisted old hand drew back the dirty blanket-door and a small, bent man shuffled into the yard.

"Abuelo?" Josh whispered. Forgetting the danger, he jumped to his feet and shouted, "Abuelo! Grand-father!" The old man turned, spotted Josh, and then hurried back into his little house.

Josh ran around the pond. As he approached the door, the old man closed the blanket-door and blocked the doorway with his body.

"Grandfather? What is it?"

"Go away from here, Hijo. This place is evil. Go away and never come back."

Chapter 4

"**G**randfather, what is going on?" Josh forced his way into the shack. The old man wasn't really his grandfather. He was actually the first convert among the local people. The man came to live at the missionary compound and became an adopted member of the family.

"Where is my father?"

"Hijo, your father has been taken by evil men. They steal people's souls with their white powder. You must leave this place before they steal yours."

"Where is my father?"

"He was up in the compound two days ago, but now, who can say. They maybe took him back to their palace. He is sick. His eyes ..."

"Where is this—"

"Joshua, leave this place! Your father is in God's hands. You must save ..." His grandfather suddenly stopped talking and put his hand over Josh's mouth. He turned his head to listen.

Josh heard singing. The same singing he had heard earlier that day. As the voices were grew louder, his grandfather motioned for him to pull the rickety old cot away from the back wall. The old man lifted a heavy, woven straw mat; his bony, twisted finger pointing at the hole beneath it. With his head he motioned for Josh to get into the dark, narrow hole.

The voices outside turned to angry shouts. They heard heavy footsteps. Someone was running toward the shack. Before Josh could think, the old man grabbed his shirt and pushed him into the hole.

Josh slid down on his back and ducked so the lid could close. His grandfather dropped the cover and pushed the cot back into place. A shower of dust settled on Josh when his grandfather sat on the cot.

Outside the door, a man started to yell. "Old man! Where are you? Where is my water! You are to have water waiting by the trail. Your life depends on water!"

Josh held his breath.

"My hearing is not so good," his grandfather said.

Josh heard his grandfather leave the room. Another man walked slowly around the tiny shack. Then a loud crash, as things were tossed and smashed about, startled Josh. He bumped his head. All of his grand-father's belongings were trashed.

Dust stirred and began to filter through the straw. Josh's nose tingled. Quietly he wiggled it back and forth to keep himself from sneezing. His body stiffened as he felt something crawl down his face. He

43

slapped his cheek but instead of insects, it was soup creeping down his face and chest. Suddenly, he was itchy all over. He wanted to reach up and wipe it off, but if he made the slightest noise, the intruder would discover his hiding place.

Josh didn't know how much longer he could stay in the hole. Darkness and dust left him restless. Just as he started to push the mat off his head, he heard his grandfather's voice.

"Do you want some water now?"

"What do you think, old man. Bring me water, now!"

"My bucket is over by your people."

Josh knew his grandfather was trying to lure the man away from the hut.

But the man kicked over the makeshift table and bench. Footsteps thumped across the room toward the cot. A few grunts later the cot was pushed into the cardboard wall of the house. Before Josh could think of what to do, the man kicked the cot.

A cloud of dust exploded into Josh's face. He blew out a puff of dust and squinted. As he tried to focus he heard the man's gruff voice.

"Get out of my way, old man!"

Josh wiped his face with both hands.

"I will get you some water," said Josh' grandfather as he left the hut.

Josh raised the mat enough to peek out. The straw covering had only moved a few inches. "That was close." With one eye he looked through a hole in the cardboard wall, and saw the same people he had seen that morning. Standing off to one side was the girl he saw crawling in the jungle. She seemed nervous and pointed her gun at his grandfather.

"Don't be late again! Useless old man!" The leader shouted as he threw a cup of water in Josh' grandfather's face.

The old man bowed and stepped away. Everyone laughed and started down the trail. Josh could feel his face grow hot with anger as he searched for something he could use as a weapon. He wanted to do something, though he knew he didn't have a chance against their guns. He had never hurt anyone intentionally, but that might change today.

He wriggled out of the hole and let the mat down without a sound. Moving to the door, he squatted on the floor and opened the hanging blanket just enough to see outside. His grandfather motioned for him to get away from the door. The group of armed people had stopped.

His grandfather busied himself by cleaning up the mess they had left behind. He tried to act like nothing was wrong as he strode slowly toward the door. Everyone in the group looked back at the shack, guns by their sides, and most of them laughing.

"What are they doing now, Hijo?" Grandfather's back was turned to the people.

"They're just standing there. One of them is

missing. I don't see their leader," Josh whispered.

"They must wait for that man."

"Who are these people, Abuelo?"

"They are drug carriers. They bring the drugs to your father's airport. From there, who knows where it goes. They are paid in cash and drugs. They think the guns makes them look tough."

"The man is back, Abuelo." Josh ducked behind the post.

The old man shuffled into the front yard and picked up his dented black pan that the man had kick across the ground. He turned and waved to the group. They answered with insults and cursing. Through a slit in the wall, Josh watched the armed group move down the trail.

"The band of fools," mumbled his grandfather.

Josh came out of the hut and followed the elderly man around the yard, helping him straighten up the mess.

"Where is my father?"

"Hijo, he is in the nest of the vipers. No one but God can help him."

"But where is he, Abuelo?"

"Joshua, you cannot do anything for him. You too will become food for the viper. Go away you cannot help him now."

"I can't leave him!"

"He may not even be alive. Go home. Don't make your mother cry twice." Grandfather turned and walked into the jungle.

Josh didn't want to hear any of this. He didn't even want to think it, but to have someone say it scared him. He walked back into the shabby hut and pulled the old, broken, wooden bench out of the corner and sat down.

What should I do now? Lord, I need your help. I have to find my dad.

Josh needed a plan to find his father, but nothing he came up with seemed right. If he were going to locate him, he would have to start where he was last seen. He went to the edge of the trees where his grandfather had disappeared and looked for him under the dark canopy.

"Abuelo? Grandfather." He yelled as loud as he thought was safe, but the old man didn't answer.

"Grandfather, I'm going to look for my father." Josh waited for an answer. When none came, he headed toward the compound. He walked without making any sounds and kept looking for any danger.

The quarter mile trip to the runway was shorter than Josh remembered, but the climb soaked his shirt with sweat. When he reached the top of the cliff, he moved off the trail and into the protection of the steamy dark green jungle.

As quietly as possible, he moved through the snarl of vines and Saw Grass. When he was twenty feet from the edge of the runway, he slithered along the ground. He moved to the side of the dirt strip and

47

concealed himself in the vine-covered brush. Slowly, he pulled a small hole in the vine so he could see.

His old home didn't look the same. Most of the buildings were torn down and jungle was beginning to swallow anything that was left. The house his family had lived in was still standing, but was badly damaged. Across the runway from the house was the hangar his father used to fix his airplanes. It seemed to be the only building in the compound not damaged.

All around the hangar, in a jumbled mess, were old fuel barrels. Next to the hangar were the remains of another of his father's dismantled airplanes.

Even the smell of the jungle was not the same. Covering the sweet and musty smell of the forest were the sickening odors of a white powder which littered the ground around the old, wooden hangar.

Carefully, Josh moved from his hiding place and walked down the edge of the runway—stooped over so the tall brush would conceal him. His torn shirt and pants were soaked with sweat; not only from the humidity but from fear itself. Every breath seemed hard labor. The muscles in his legs cramped, his shoulders ached. And the fear of so many unknowns tightened his heart.

The breeze was no help at all. The only thing it did, was move the loose tin on the tumbled down roofs of the buildings. Every time the metal roof squeaked, Josh ducked for cover and scanned beyond the runway for any gunman on patrol. When he was sure no one was there, he came out of hiding and continued slowly down the side of the hard-packed airstrip.

Another shock came as he reached the old family house. One side of the roof had caved in. Screen windows were torn or missing. The house seemed haunted, especially with his mother's curtains in shreds, and fluttering in the breeze. Furniture was stacked in a pile on the front yard. Someone had tried to burn it, but a sudden jungle downpour must have doused the flames.

Leaving the runway, Josh stumbled through the underbrush toward the rear of the house. He cautiously approached the porch, backing up against the wall of the house near a window and peered over the edge of the wooden frame.

He hardly recognized the room. Everything was broken or gone. Even the white kitchen sink had been shattered, its pieces thrown around the cluttered room.

Josh tiptoed up the back steps. He was so busy trying not to be heard, he didn't see the bottle until he sent it sailing across the room with his foot.

The crash of glass breaking as it hit the stove, sent the birds and monkeys into a screaming rage. Chaos lasted for a few seconds, then fell silent as if time in the whole jungle stopped. The eerie silence sent Josh flying out the back door and into the underbrush.

He would have stayed in the forest all night, but the pounding rain forced him back into the house. Warily, he made his way through the broken-down house and headed for his old bedroom. The setting sun crept into the jumbled interior of the house. It was almost pleasant.

His bedroom, in the front of the house, was the only room that still had its roof. And the window faced the runway and the hangar.

As darkness grew and rain continued its assault, Josh decided to rest here for the night. Like all the other rooms, the furniture was either gone or broken. The woolen army blanket, crumpled in a corner, reminded him of his dad. He shook the blanket looking for scorpions and spiders.

Leaning back into the corner, sitting on top of the scratchy, green blanket, he wiped a few tears from his face. *Oh Dad, where are you?* The tears loosened much of the grime.

Yet through the tears, Josh notices a small piece of paper in the center of the floor. At first he tried to ignore it, but then, as tired as he was, crawled across the floor to pick up the tiny scrap. He recognized the paper and the print. It was all that was left of his Bible. He would have to use one of his precious matches to read the words.

When he untied the arms of the jacket knotted around his waist, the stale smell of mildew filled the room. Josh unzipped the inside pocket and pulled out the matches. He struck the match across the floor. A flame lit the room. Josh had the paper close to his face. All he could make out was "... as soon as the pursuer had gone out the ..." Something brown covered the rest.

Quickly he turned the scrap of paper over just as the light started to dim. He only caught the words "... commanded you? Be strong and ..." The flame flickered and the room went black. Be strong. That phrase was all he needed. It was etched in his thoughts now. Fumbling in the darkness, he lit up another match. The little piece of paper was still clutched in his hand.

The second match provided the light he needed to read this small portion of scripture: "Be strong and courageous. Do not be terrified; do not be discouraged, for the Lord your God will be with you ..." The rest was missing.

He knew that message was for him. He knew that verse was from the Bible, but he didn't know where. Josh closed his eyes. "Dear God, my dad says that you do things like this. I mean this verse from the Bible. Lord, I don't know what to do next. Please guide me. Amen. Oh, and help me be brave." After he opened his eyes he slipped the piece of scripture into the match case.

For the first time in two days he felt safe. He didn't know if it was his old, familiar room, God's presence, or both. His thoughts were interrupted by a few giant raindrops landing on the metal roof just before another downpour. Listening to the roar of the waters on the roof, he settled back into the corner and fell asleep.

Chapter 5

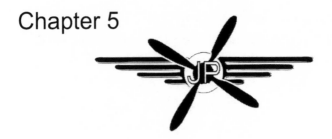

J osh didn't realize he had fallen asleep until something jerked his body off the floor, and a strong hand clamped over his mouth. He couldn't see his attacker in the dark, or hear him because of the roaring rain. The only thing he was aware of was the strength in the arm that pinned both of his to his sides and the vise-like grip on his mouth.

"What is your name?" A harsh whisper breathed directly into his ear. The smell of bad breath and body odor was overwhelming.

Josh coughed. The man's arm slammed tighter across his chest.

"What is your name? When I take my hand off your mouth you will tell me your name!" The man took his grimy hand off Josh' mouth.

"You speak English?" The powerful grip left Josh out of breath.

"Your
name!"

"Josh ... Joshua Powers."

"Josh? Joshua Powers?" The man repeated the

name, this time much kinder.

Josh tried to focus. His attacker looked like a character from a nightmare: long stringy hair, straggly beard, he was filthy, his breath foul, and his body smelled like he had skipped a thousand baths. The longer he looked at the dirty face the more he started to recognize the eyes.

"Mr. Logan? Is that you?"

"Joshua Powers!" The man's breath-stopping grip turned into a gentle hug. "I thought you weren't coming."

"What happened here?"

Randy Logan had been Josh' idol while he was growing up. Logan was one of the missionary pilots who had flown with his dad. Josh remembered how neat the man had always looked. When everyone else was covered with sweat, Logan seemed to be cool and starched.

"What happened to you?" Josh' eyes were glued on Logan's appearance.

"It's a disguise, Joshua. I want the drug dealers to think I'm crazy."

"Crazy? Why?"

"Josh." Logan stared at the ground. "I'm the guy the drug dealer wants. I work for the Drug Enforcement Agency."

"You what? You let them take my father?"

"I wasn't here when they kidnapped him. They came in the middle of the night and took him to the

Palace."

"The Palace? Where is this Palace?"

"It's about fifteen miles north of here. There's an airport there and your dad is being held in one of the hangars."

"If you know where he is, why don't you tell them you are the DEA man?"

"It's not that easy. Your dad won't let me. He wants to make sure that we put these guys out of business."

"How do you know all this?"

"Joshua, I take him food and talk to him every few days. He knows God is going to deliver him."

"You what? Do they just let you walk in and talk to him?"

"That's where my disguise comes in. They call me El Americano loco—the crazy American. I got the idea from the Bible."

"You did?"

"Do you remember King David? Once when he was afraid Saul was going to kill him, he fled to the city of Gath. The king of Gath was Achish and one of his servants recognized David."

"What did he do?"

"When the servant told King Achish, that frightened David even more. So David pretended to be insane. He would stand by the gate of the city and scratch it with his fingernails. The Bible says he let drool run down into his beard."

"What'd the King do?"

"The servant must have taken David to the king. But when the king saw David acting weird and drooling on himself, he got mad at the servant."

"Did he let David go?"

Logan spoke in a deep voice as if he were the king. "The king was mad. He said 'Look at that man! He's insane! Am I so short of madmen that you have to bring this fellow here to carry on like this in front of me?'"

They both chuckled then fell silent.

"I run around the jungle screaming at night. They think I'm crazy and they shoot to scare me away. When I go see your dad, I stand out in the jungle behind the hangar and yell. They think I am insulting him. After they have their laughs, and shoot their guns into the trees, I crawl up to the back of the hangar and talk with him."

"Is he okay?"

"You know your dad. He never complains about anything. When I leave him, I usually feel better."

"When did you see him last?"

"I saw him here two days ago. He was waiting for you. Say, where's your airplane? I didn't see it out front."

"It's ... it's in the river. I had a little accident."

"You been in the city so long you forgot about runways? Anyway, your dad looks tired, but he's fine."

"Where's your family?" Josh tried to change the

55

subject to a happier one.

Logan slumped back against the wall and sighed. "They're a few miles from here, living in a cave like animals. I've got to get them out."

"Why didn't they leave with my mother?"

"We thought they would be safe. But these men are crazy. They would take my wife and oldest daughter and do what they wanted. I've got to get them out."

"Won't the DEA help you?"

"I can't risk the contact right now. When we get your dad out of the hangar, I'll send them all out with you."

Josh looked at Logan. Logan smiled and Josh was grateful he had help to rescue his dad. Randy Logan knew the jungle both from the air and the ground and with his help, he felt sure his dad would be free in a few days.

"Get some sleep, Joshua. We have some hard days ahead of us." Logan slid down flat on the floor and turned his back.

Josh lay down and snuggled his head into the old musty army blanket. After a few seconds Josh asked, "How did you get in with the DEA?"

"I was approached by a man over in the Capital. At first he would ask if I saw anything unusual from the sky. Next thing I knew I was involved." Logan stopped talking for a bit when they heard the deep rumble of a twin engine airplane taxing on the dirt runway. "Must be about 4:00 AM." Logan moved to the edge of the window in the front of Josh's room. "They always come at the same time. By sunup they'll have the plane loaded with drugs and take off for the Palace."

Josh checked his watch. It was 4:05 AM.

"That plane goes to the Palace?" Logan put his hand on Josh' shoulder.

"Don't even think about it. You hear me? These people are not normal. It's not safe."

"But I thought you said you wanted to get my dad?"

"No Joshua. No way! Don't even make a sound until that airplane leaves in the morning. Go back to sleep. I'll go do my act in the jungle and come back and take you to my family when they're gone. You'll be safe there." Then Logan disappeared into the darkness.

Josh only had to wait a few minutes for Logan's first scream. It sent Josh into shivers even though he knew where it came from. The scream was the cross between a terrified woman and a wounded animal, followed by a hideous laugh.

The men around the airplane didn't like the sound either. Several armed men ran to the edge of the runway and fired their automatic weapons into the sky. When they stopped firing they stood guard while other men loaded the plane.

Five minutes passed before Logan let out his second volley of tortured moans and sounds. This time it came from the opposite side of the hangar.

The gunmen ran to the other side, shouted

some-thing and began firing high into the trees. When the shooting stopped, the jungle was silent. Josh waited for more screams, but they never came.

His heart sank as he imagined the worst. Fear, like a slithering snake, crept up his back. His mind raced from one thing to the next. Finally, he remembered his verse.

Locating his leather jacket on the floor, Josh removed the torn piece of paper from the match case. As he watched the men loading the airplane, he read the verse: "Be strong and courageous. For the Lord is with me."

The words seemed to calm him. He chuckled a little, and shook his head, when he remembered that two days before he didn't even think about God, let alone talk to Him.

Josh spent the few remaining minutes of the pre-dawn grey light trying to memorize his Bible verse. He sat by the window, watching these criminals load the bundles of drugs into his dad's old airplane. He would say the verse every time he started to fall asleep. He prayed silently, hoping that the last bursts of gunfire had not found their target.

By the time the grey had turned to a bright red dawn, Joshua could repeat the verse without any help from the small piece of paper. He slipped it back inside the container.

Josh hadn't thought about the Bible since he was twelve years old, and now his whole Bible was a tiny scrap of paper that only had part of one verse.

For a few moments the sun broke through the space between the ground and the thick, black layer of clouds. A bright beam of sunlight filled the room. The morning light would give him a new beginning.

The me finished loading the airplane and one large man, with a big belly, locked the door of the hangar where the drugs were stored. He walked halfway to the plane, turned, and looked at the door. After staring a few seconds, he walked back and checked the lock again. Two men followed him and stood guard. Josh remembered how these men had fired their weapons into the dark jungle at a mere sound.

He remembered Logan telling him that this airplane went to the Palace. Without thinking what might happen, Josh jumped to his feet and grabbed his leather jacket. He straightened his dirty hair, and wiped the toes of both boots on the back of his pants legs.

Having groomed himself the best he could, he went out the back door of the old house and started to make as much noise as he could as he walked to the runway. Even with all of his noise, no one spotted him. When he reached the center of the runway, one of the gunmen walked away from the airplane.

"Hey! Am I glad to see you guys," Josh yelled. The gunman shouted something in Spanish. Three other men appeared and ran toward him, aiming their guns.

"On the ground!" A voice boomed from behind the airplane.

"Hi, I'm Joshua Powers. I'm here to pick up my dad." His voice was shaky as he lowered himself to the ground.

"On your face," said the overweight man walking toward him.

Josh lay down on the muddy runway. The men formed a circle as the chubby man came and stood by. Josh could only hear him.

"Check the kid out."

One of the men handed off his weapon and searched Josh from head to foot. He took Josh' wallet out of his pocket and handed it to the large man.

"So you are Joshua Powers. Where have you been?"

"I had a little plane trouble and landed it in the river."

"So, you are the pigeon I shot from the sky."

All the men laughed. The large man threw the wallet onto his back. But the one who had searched him, grabbed it and before stuffing the wallet back into Josh's pocket, took the two hundred dollars—money Josh' mother had given him.

"Get up, Pigeon." The big one said.

"Is my dad still here?" Josh tried to sound as innocent as he could.

"Your Dad? We don't know him. What is his

name?"

"Doug Powers. I was supposed to meet him here two or three days ago."

"But I shot you down, Pigeon."

The man was starting to annoy Josh.

"Pigeon, your padre is a guest ... of my employer."

For the first time Josh looked straight into the man's face. His blue eyes and dirty, long blonde hair surprised Josh. The heavy man's double chins, jiggled as he spoke.

"We would be glad to take you to him ... For a price, of course."

"He took all of my money." Josh pointed at the man who had searched him.

The man took out the bills and waved it in Josh's face. But the big man grabbed the money from the gunman's hand and raised his fist like he was going to strike him. "Plane leaves in five minutes. Don't miss it." He turned and walked toward the plane. The seat of his pants hung down below his knees and the center seam was ripped open. The man was so large that two of the gunmen had to help him through the rear door of the airplane. Everyone else scurried around preparing for take-off.

Someone put the barrel of his gun in Josh's back and pushed him toward the plane.

Once inside, two things surprised Josh. The plane was filled to the top with large bundles, wrapped in burlap, and the large man was in the pilot's seat. Sticking his head into the cockpit, Josh could see the man's belly pushing against the control wheel of the airplane.

"Sit down and keep out of the way," said one of the gunmen.

Josh moved back by the opened doorway near the tail. Both sides of the door were guarded, each man with a gun and each man staring into the sky.

The high-pitched whine of the starter made Josh tense up. He really didn't want to make this trip. The plane was loaded too heavy, and he had doubts about the pilot. The first engines roaring to life only made his fears worse.

The second engine backfired a few times then started. The old airplane moved slowly toward the opposite end of the field. He thought about jumping through the open door while the plane was taxing, but he wanted to find his dad and was afraid that men would shoot him.

As he looked into the jungle, some movement caught his eye. His eyes search again, but saw nothing. Just as the plane reached the end of the runway, and started to swing around, Logan charged from the underbrush moaning and screaming.

Josh was as surprised as the guards. Logan looked much worse in the light. His pants were shredded in long strips up to the waist and his shirt only had sleeves attached to the back. His hair was matted and his gray beard hung halfway down his chest in long, stringy curls.

Both of the guards pulled back behind the edge of the door. The one next to Josh raised his weapon to shoot. Josh pushed the man's arm to mess up his aim and almost fell out the door. The bullets strayed far above Logan's head, and he disappeared into the thick dark green brush.

Josh started to mumble an apology, but the man grabbed him by the shirt and shoved him toward the front of the plane. The force knocked him off his feet, and he landed on the cool aluminum floor between the bags of drugs.

"Don't do that again, kid, or you will die!" Josh didn't look at the man again.

Chapter 6

The two engines of the Beech 18 popped and sputtered as the overweight pilot pushed the curved throttle handles forward. Both engines roared as the plane began to move slowly down the runway—with big soft tires it was like rolling on a mattress.

The plane's bounce worsened as it gained speed. Josh wondered if it could clear the trees at the end of the runway over Malo Falls. He moved to the rear of the plane to sit near the door.

Slowly, the tail lifted off the ground. Through the open door, he could see the trees rushing toward the plane like a giant green tidal wave.

"Abort! Abort the take off! We're not going to make it!" Josh screamed before he could control himself. He raced toward the cockpit. But before he took three steps, one of the gunmen slammed him back into the corner.

"Sit down, kid. El Gordo knows what he is doing."

"We're going to hit the trees!"

"Quiet! And stay in that corner!"

Through a window, Josh watched the plane close in on the trees. With its excess weight it seemed the plane was just hanging on the propellers.

"See, I told you he knew—" The man's sentence was cut short by a loud scream from the cockpit. The airplane crashed through the tops of the trees. A spray of propeller-chopped leaves and twigs slammed into the sides of the plane, and a shower of wet green mulch came flying through the open door. The plane shuddered as it skimmed the treetops.

Both gunmen were covered with a thick, green, smelly, liquid from the tropical trees the airplane had just trimmed. Josh spit some tree parts out of his mouth. Suddenly, the plane made a sharp left turn.

Through the open door, he could see the top of Malo Falls as it passed sixty feet below. One of the gunmen slid on the slick floor toward the door as the plane made its steep bank. The other man tried to stop him, but they both began a deadly slide toward the trees below. Josh grabbed a tie-down ring in the floor and stretched his legs out toward the men.

"Grab my feet!"

One of the clawing hands latched on to his leg like a vise. With his other hand, the man grabbed the collar of his friend's shirt just as his feet went out the door. The man slid halfway out; his hands desperately reaching for something to grab. His life hung by the collar of his shirt.

Josh cringed with excruciating pain as the man's fingers dug into his flesh. He wanted to kick the hand off with his free foot, but he knew it would kill both men. Then just when he thought he couldn't stand the pain any longer, he felt his hand slip on the ring.

His fingers were gradually sliding off the cold, metal ring which was covered with the wet, green slime from the trees. He realized he was in as much danger as the men who clung to his leg. He looked at the man hanging out of the door, and saw nothing but terror on his face. His eyes pleading with Josh to save him.

"I can't hold ..." Josh stopped and remembered the last part of his verse. "The Lord is with me," he whispered under his breath. "The Lord is with me!" he shouted.

Josh jerked his arm enough to regain his life-saving grip on the wet ring. Both men screamed when Josh moved his leg, and the man dug his fingers deeper Josh gasped.

Then finally, the plane returned to level flight. And with some of the pressure off, the man hanging out of the door was able to grab a corner of a burlap bag with one hand. They all worked together and pulled the man back inside the plane. Like rats on a sinking ship, they scurried to the pile of cargo. There they held tight onto the ropes as far away from the door as possible.

Just when they got the chance to relax, the overweight pilot shouted out new orders. One gunmen went to the front of the plane. His hand never left the ropes that held the cargo. He came back to relay the order. "El Gordo says we must lighten the load. Kid, go untie those bails and throw them out. Those by the door."

Josh stared at the man like he was crazy.

"Move kid, or I'll give you a flying lesson." His head motioned toward the door.

Josh held the ropes that bound the load and steadied himself. Suddenly the airplane banked to the left and sent his feet skidding across the floor. Then quickly the plane leveled off again. The pilot and one of the gunmen roared with laughter.

Pulling himself to his feet, Josh moved toward the last bundles. He climbed over the load and got away from the open door. Lying on top of the bundles, he untied the knot that held them in place. When he had a long length of rope, he fastened one end to a tie-down ring in the floor and the other end around his waist.

"Throw the bundles out, pigeon!" The pilot looked over his shoulders.

"Be courageous, the Lord is with me," Josh said to himself. He got himself around the bags on the floor which was as slippery as ice. Holding onto a burlap bag and shoved it toward the door.

When he was near the door, the pilot smirked and pushed one of the rudder pedals so the airplane skidded sideways. Another roar of laughter came from the front.

Pushing the large bundle out the door, Josh

watched as it fell away and exploded in a white cloud on the river bank. He thought the more bags he threw off the plane, the less the drug dealers would have left to sell. That made him work faster.

After shoving two more bundles out the door, Josh felt someone move close behind him. It was the man whose life he saved. He was tying a rope around his waist–and started to help Josh with the bundles. When he and Josh bent over to lift the same bag, the man leaned close to Josh' ear. "Muchas gracias, hijo," he whispered. Then he grabbed the bundle by himself and threw it out the door.

Josh tried not to act surprised.

Finally, the pilot yelled that they had thrown enough of the profits out of the door. Josh left his safety line tied to his waist and sat down. He felt better being away from the gunmen. The man who had helped him, sat down next to him.

"What is your name, hijo?"

"Joshua. My friends ..." Josh stopped himself. This man was not a friend. This man had kidnapped his father and had shot at Randy Logan just a few minutes before. "What's your name?"

After a long pause the man replied. "In this business you don't tell people your name, but you can call me Juan."

Josh knew it wasn't his real name, but it helped having something to call him. It made him feel less alone. They sat staring into the vast, dark green jungle without saying another word.

A few minutes later Juan pushed on Josh' arm and pointed out the door. "Look. There is the camp of those stone-age devils."

"The what?"

"The Alasa," Juan said. "They sneak up and put one of their spears in your back. You don't even hear them."

Josh leaned as far out of the door as he could. In the center of the camp was the ring of spears the Alasa always had ready. An Indian with a blue baseball cap ran from one of the huts, grabbed a spear on the run and threw it at the plane.

The other gunmen came back to the door and shot his automatic weapon at him. "Mindless savage does that every time. One of these days I will teach him a lesson."

Both spear and bullets missed their targets.

The engines of the old airplane slowed to an idle. Josh looked into the cockpit to see if something was wrong. As the plane turned, he saw a new paved runway cut out of the jungle. When the flaps went down and slowed the plane, he realized they were going to land.

He quickly looked out to find the Alasa village and checked the time on his watch. He estimated the speed of the plane, and calculated the village was five miles from this airport.

Then without trying to create too much

69

attention, he moved to the other side of the plane where he could see the sun through a window. With his watch, he figured that the Indian village was southwest through very dense forest: a two-hour trip.

The plane turned toward the runway, gliding gently through the still morning air. The big, soft tires squealed as they made contact with the new black top. The plane bounced once, then settled onto the runway. After a long taxi and several turns, the pilot killed the engines and the plane rolled to a stop beside a small business jet. On the side of the jet, in large gold letters, were written the words, "The Gates of Hell."

Josh untied the safety line from his waist and jumped out. Walking slowly around to the other side of the jet, he planned to slip off into the jungle.

"Pigeon!" bellowed the pilot. "Where do you think you are going? You must wait here for your ride to the Palace."

"I thought I would walk. I need the exercise."

"Nice try, kid." The pilot gave a hearty belly laugh as he walked to the shady side of the plane. He leaned against the cool, dirty metal. "Kid. Come here where I can see you."

Reluctantly, Josh walked toward him.

"Sit here on the ground next to my feet." The pilot pointed his chubby finger to a grease spot on the tarmac.

Josh didn't want to sit to sit in the oil. It would ruin his clothes. But then he looked himself over. His shirt was shredded with hundreds of tiny slits from the Saw grass. His pants were a deep rust color from the river water, and the bottom of one pant leg was ripped off and sagged down around the top of his boot. The leather flight jacket he loved so much, smelled like mildew and was still wet. Deciding that nothing else could hurt his clothes, Josh lower to the dirty asphalt.

The big pilot didn't look any better. His clothes were filthy and baggy. The soles of his shoes were worn through and he had squashed down the heel so he could slide his bare feet into them like slippers.

Josh could smell sweat, dirt, oil, and human waste. He untied the arms of his jacket, and pulled it across his nose; thankful the smell was not coming from him. Slowly, he slid slowly away from the man.

"Don't move, Kid!"

"Car's coming," interrupted Juan.

Josh walked to where Juan was standing. Juan pointed up the freshly paved road. A bent, old, rusty army truck pulled up and screeched to a stop in front of them. Behind the wheel was an older, distinguish man in a butler's uniform.

"Where's the limo?" shouted the pilot.

"I thought this was the proper vehicle in which to haul swine," said the driver. "Who is this urchin you have with you?"

"Joshua Powers," Josh answered.

"Charmed, I'm sure. Get in the back all of you."

Josh climbed into the back of the truck and sat

as far from the sleazy pilot as he could.

"We shouldn't be treated this way. Mr. Martinez will hear about this." The pilot was grumbling as he struggled to get into the truck.

"Yes. Quite," said the butler as he gave the pilot a look of disgust and started the engine. The old truck rattled up the road with an ear-splitting sound, punctuated by the grinding of shifting gears.

The road through the jungle was smooth and pleasant, and a heavy tree canopy shaded the open truck. Once the truck reached the top of the hill, the driver placed a call on his cell, then laid down the phone and turned to the pilot smiling a menacing smile.

The road continued over another ~~small~~ hill and into a beautiful valley where the jungle had all been cleared. In the middle of the clearing sat the Palace.

Josh could hardly believe his eyes. It was a large, three storied house with a porch running all the way around. Outside the porch was a mote with a small drawbridge. In front was a beautiful flower garden with a large pool in the center. When the squeaky, old truck pulled up to the bridge, two armed guards stepped onto the road.

"Who is this boy?" asked a man dressed in a black suit and sunglasses.

"Joshua Powers," said the old driver. "He won't be with us long."

Josh didn't like the sound of that.

72

The guard stepped out of the way and the truck lurched ahead. Pulling up to the side of the house, the driver brought the rattling truck to a stop.

"Wait here, all of you." The old driver slid out of the driver's seat and disappeared into the house.

The other men crawled out of the back and stood nearby. The pilot was still grumbling and kicking the ground when Juan nudged him. All three men turned to face the porch. The overweight pilot took a step forward and bowed. He opened his mouth to speak, but was cut off.

"Don't you ever bathe, pig?" said a voice from the porch.

The pilot bowed again and backed away as a small, handsome man in a white suit appeared from the beautiful, white porch. In one hand he clutched a handkerchief which he placed over his mouth when the smell of the pilot reached him. "Get out of my sight." He dismissed the pilot with a wave of his hand.

The pilot and the other two men hurried toward the back of the house. Josh was left with the man in the white suit.

"I am Carlos Martinez. Who are you? And why are you an uninvited guest at my home?

"I am Joshua Powers. I'm here to pick up my father. Is he still here?

"What is his name?"

"Doug Powers. He was the missionary who was kidnapped by some drug dealers." It all came out

73

before Josh could stop himself.

The man's black eyes flamed with rage. "How dare you accuse me of such a crime in my own home." He spun around and stomped back into the house.

Fear crept through Josh' body like a cold fog. Within seconds, two men in black suits came out of the house pointing their guns at him. Their wrap-around sunglasses concealed their eyes. One of them smelled of a sweet aftershave lotion.

Josh didn't move a muscle. Fear mixed with aftershave equaled nausea. He forced himself to think of his verse. All he could remember now was, "I am with you."

Josh jumped when the old butler spoke. "I told you, you wouldn't be staying long." He leaned over to one of the guards and whispered in his ear.

The guard thrust the barrel of his gun into Josh' side and pushed him toward the back of the house. "You will pay for that insult, you dog. And so will your father."

Chapter 7

"Is my father here?" Joshua looked from the face of one guard to the other. The men looked at each other, but didn't answer.

"Where is he?" asked Josh.

"Your father is ... you will see him in time," snapped the older of the two gunmen. "Now, walk. That way." The guard waved his gun around.

Josh could see a small dirt trail leading down the hill, and disappearing into the jungle. He pulled his tattered shirtsleeve up so he could see his watch, and glanced at the sun to check the direction they were going. They were heading west, back toward the airport.

He thought about what the gunmen might do to his father for the things he said to Carlos Martinez? The TV news at home had been full of the exploits of Carlos Martinez: the notorious drug Czar of El Salvador. There were never any pictures of him, so Josh imagined Martinez was a large muscled man with fangs, who never bathed and kicked small children. What he looked like in real life made him laugh. Carlos Martinez was a small, pale man who was afraid of getting dirty.

A sharp jab in the ribs brought him back to the present.

"What are you smiling at, boy? Are you having a good time? You won't think it's funny when Mr. Martinez gets done with you."

Josh held his aching side and tried to walk faster down the trail. He knew that Carlos Martinez' power came from men like these who could be paid to do anything. Without the millions of dollars he made from the illegal sale of drugs, Carlos Martinez would be just another poor, powerless farmer trying to make enough money to live. But Martinez could afford all the evil that money could buy.

The loud, rattling, cracks of automatic gunfire froze Josh in his tracks and set the jungle birds into a screaming frenzy.

"What do you think you are doing? Are you trying to escape?" The guard panted for air between words.

Slowly Josh turned around and realized while he was deep in thought, he had moved too far ahead of his guards.

"Don't try that again."

The threat was enough to make him feel sick. Maybe his mother had been right. Someone else should have come and pretended to be Joshua Powers. Someone who was braver and who would have brought his father safely home.

"Be strong and courageous," Josh mumbled to himself. "Be strong and courageous for the Lord your God will be with you wherever you go." He repeated that verse several more times.

With the morning sun jungle steam began to rise. His own body now smelled like mildew. The guards talked in Spanish and laughed at the way Josh looked and smelled.

The lush, green trees, towering high above their heads, fell silent. Gone were the usual chatter of birds and monkeys. Only the cruel laughter and taunts of the guards remained.

Silence always made Joshua uneasy. Tolando had taught him to listen to the trees. When the trees became silent, there was danger.

The dark jungle trail made a sharp turn and went up a hill. When they had crossed the top of the hill one of the guards started shouting. The noises in the trees erupted like an explosion. All of the birds started to squawk in reply. Josh stopped and waited.

"Boy, you better not try to—" The rest was drowned out by the noise of the birds.

"You don't even have enough sense to run away." The younger guard talked on, but Josh didn't listen. He was waiting to hear the trees become deadly silent again.

"Get moving. We will wait for the old man by the stream."

Josh thought how sad it was that these people

didn't even respect each other. They were only together because of the false power of money and guns.

When they turned the corner in the trail, Josh' eyes fell on the bright, red feather on the end of a wooden shaft. He stopped and knelt.

"What are you doing?" Snapped the guard.

"There!" Josh pointed at the spear.

The guard grabbed Josh's shirt collar and pushed him to the ground. "Get down, boy! Get down!" Fear was in the guard's eyes. The man pressed his expensive suit into the smelly, decaying leaves. Josh could tell the guard knew exactly what the spear meant.

"Stay right behind me." The guard crawled farther off the trail.

Josh started to slide on his belly when his eye caught something bright blue on the ground next to the spear. "My hat. How'd that get there?"

"Shut up, you fool. These savages will kill you for fun."

The guard, who had been so brave with his powerful automatic weapon pointed at a fourteen-year-old kid, was sweating; his face, pale. The stone-aged Alasa were more powerful than his gun.

Josh lay staring at the hat. It had washed off his head when he had jumped into the river to escape the panther. He thought he saw one of the Alasa Indians wearing it when the plane passed over their village. An Alasa had tried to warn him to stay away from the missionary compound. Maybe Tolando. The possibilities raced through his head.

"That hat was a gift," Josh said as he got to his feet.

"Down, you fool! They will see you!"

"They already see us. They know exactly where we are." Josh walked over to the spear and picked up the hat. Checking inside, he looked for the familiar label that his mother sewed inside all of his clothes. There in his mom's beautiful cross-stitch was his name. When he put it on his head, Josh smelled that familiar scent of the Alasa. They used the sap from a big yellow flower to make themselves smell better.

"Yep. It's my hat. It's a gift to me. I'm not in danger, you are." Josh slipped the hat onto his head and walked over to where the gunman was hiding.

The man reached up, grabbed his belt and jerked Josh to the ground. "You are still in danger. From me!" He pulled his bright purple handkerchief from his pocket and tied Josh's hands behind his back. Then he took Josh's belt, bound his feet, and fastened them to the purple silk.

"Now try to get away," the guard whispered. He got into a crouched position, and started running back down the trail.

Josh' face pressed against the cool, damp ground. He heard nothing. He moaned from the pain in his shoulder and knees. He wiggled around, trying to take some of the pressure off, but the movement only made things worse.

"Be courageous. I'm with you."

Then, when he thought he couldn't stand the pain any longer, the belt binding his feet and hands came loose. Josh looked around but saw nobody. Straightening his legs eased the pain. He rolled from his stomach to his side and quickly looked down the trail.

A sudden burst of rapid gunfire sent the birds screeching. Within seconds the guard came running down the trail shooting aimlessly into the jungle.

Breathless, the guard fell to the ground beside Josh. "They took him. Those heathens took Norberto. We will be next." He rolled Josh back onto his stomach. When he saw the belt hanging from the silk handkerchief, he grabbed both of the guns and again shot wildly into the trees. "They cut the belt. The belt has been cut!" He dropped one gun and pulled off the pieces of the belt which had held Josh's feet. "Hurry, we are in danger. We must run to the airport."

"I don't think I'm in danger," Josh said. "They would have killed me instead of cutting the belt."

That response seemed to push the man over the edge and into a panic. Jumping to his feet, he yanked Josh upright by the handkerchief that bound his hands behind him.

"Ouch!" Josh cried out.

The guard wrapped one arm around Josh's neck. "If they don't want to kill you, they won't hurt me while I'm this close to you." He shoved Josh down the trail.

They stumbled through the jungle together. But after twenty steps or so, their feet somehow got tangled and both tumbled to the ground. One of the guns hit Josh square on the forehead. A large lump appeared instantly.

The guard climbed to his feet and jerked Josh up. He removed the clip of ammunition from one of the guns and threw the gun into the underbrush. Carefully he slipped the ammo into his pocket, then pushed Josh down the path; the muzzle of his gun on the back of Josh' head. "Just walk slow and stay on the trail. No tricks." The guard growled; his eyes widened, his eyebrows raised, and he looked from side to side and over his shoulder. The man's fear scared Joshua more than anything.

"I think you are right," said Josh. "I think you will be safe as long as I am safe."

"Quiet! Just keep moving." He moved a little closer to Josh.

Eventually the sound of the jungle returned with the chirping of birds and the chatter of monkeys. The path was winding gently downhill, so they picked up the pace. His guard didn't seem to mind now. When they reached a small log footbridge, Josh was ordered to stop.

"Pasillo!" the guard shouted. Silence. He tried again. "Pasillo! Pasillo, Pasillo!"

"What does Pasillo mean?" asked Josh.

"Passage," came a soft voice from behind them.

"That is our code word." The guard spun around and banged his gun on a tree.

The man with the soft voice started to laugh. "What has happened to you, Amigo? You look like you have been living with pigs."

"The Alasa have taken Norberto. I had to hide for my life."

"With some pigs?" The man's laughter was infectious.

Josh looked at this once mighty guard and almost laughed. His suit was caked with mud and his perfect hair matted and wet with sweat. His shiny shoes were covered in sludge and his wet socks bagged down around his ankles. Anger flamed in the guard's eyes as he stepped over to Josh and stuck the barrel of his gun in his mouth.

"Silence! You may not live to see your father."

"Take the boy to the hangar, and when you return I'll loan you a shoe brush," said the man with the soft voice, as he walked away … still laughing. The birds seemed to join in.

As the guard pushed Josh across the bridge, Josh lost his footing and plunged headfirst onto the path.

"Get up, pig." The fear was gone, and the guard was back in charge.

Josh struggled to his feet the best he could with his hands tied behind his back. The guard didn't help.

"Move! Now!" His tone reflected his anger.

Josh walked the direction the man motioned. Five minutes later they came to the edge of the runway. Josh looked around. To his right, he could see the shiny business jet and his dad's dirty, old Beech 18. To his left was a metal hangar with fuel barrels stacked against the side.

The guard pushed him toward a small door in the side of the hangar. The sun was high and hot, and oil on the asphalt was sticking to his shoes. The heat coming off the black surface made him sweat. He was glad to finally get to the shade of the hangar.

But there, near the door, Josh was shoved against the wall ... face first. The guard pulled out a small, golden chain with a brass key which was hanging around his neck. He unlocked the paddle lock, and kicked the door open.

Hot, stale air escaped through the door. Josh moved quickly before the man could push him again. The hangar was dark. They both had trouble seeing inside. Josh tripped on something and once again fell face first. This time into a smelly, stagnant puddle of water. With his hands tied behind his back, he managed to roll over on his side, and tried to sit up.

"You can wait here for your father."

"Could you untie my hands? Hey!"

But the guard slammed the door shut. Now it was pitch black. Josh closed his eyes and waited for them to adjust. Then, as he lay on the sloppy floor, he heard a soft sound.

"Who's there?" Josh held his breath. "Hello. Who's there?" He could hear someone shuffling on the floor. He struggled to turn himself over to face whoever was in the room with him. In the dim light, Josh could see an outline of the person.

"Who are you?" he asked again.

The figure moved across the room and passed through a shaft of light coming through a hole in the roof. Josh caught a glimpse of a very hairy man in tattered clothes.

"Logan? Is that you?"

The person stopped, and turned toward Josh. Gradually the figure approached the spot where Josh lay on the floor.

"Logan? Is that you? You're not scaring me."

The shadowy form moved stuck out his hand. The hand waved around in the air until it came to rest on Josh's hip.

"Get your hands off me. Get away from me." Josh tried to wriggle away, but the man grabbed Josh' shirt, and his hand traced over Josh' side until it found his face. Josh turned as far as he could to avoid the touch, but it followed toward Josh' right cheek.

"What is your name?" The voice was soft and raspy.

"Joshua Powers ... I came to get my dad."

"Oh dear Lord. Thank you! I have been rescued."

"Dad?"

The man pulled Josh's face up near his and kissed him on the forehead.

"Dad. It *is* you!"

Chapter 8

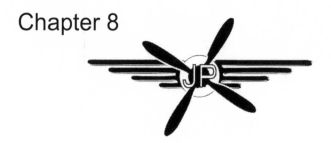

D oug Powers reached over his son's body
and fumbled with the silk handkerchief
that tied Josh' hands. The knot was too wet so, for now,
he couldn't get it untied.

Josh' father helped him to his feet and wrapped
his arms around him. "I'm so glad to see you," Doug
Powers whispered. "They told me you had crashed in
the jungle."

"I'm glad I found you. Everyone kept telling me
they didn't know you."

His dad hugged him again.

"Dad, do you have something to cut the handkerchief?"

"Oh. Oh yes."

Josh's father walked toward the side of the large
room. Josh waited for his eyes to adjust to the darkness
and followed along.

"I saw Randy yesterday," Josh said. "He told me
not to go with these guys, but they brought me to you."

His dad spun him around by the shoulders and looked him in the eyes. "Son, don't trust those guys. Everything about them is a lie."

They shuffled over to his bed on top of some old packing crates.

"Randy brought me a knife awhile back. That will do the job on these ropes." His hand searched over his bed and followed the blanket to the wall. He moved it slowly back and forth until he found a post; followed the post up to a tiny shelf and picked up the knife. "Ah. Here it is. Now let's get those ropes off your hands."

Josh turned around. His father ran his hand from the shoulder down Josh' arm until he found the silk handkerchief. Carefully, he cut the silk that bound Josh' hands. Josh stretched his arms forward; both the muscle in his shoulder and back ached.

"Randy should be here tonight. He comes every three days or so."

"I don't know, Dad. He tried to stop me from going with the smugglers and they shot at him. They might have hit him."

"Did you see him fall?"

"No, he just kinda disappeared."

"That's our Randy." Doug Powers laughed softly. "They didn't get him. He'll be here tonight. Joshua, I'm sure glad you're here."

Josh stared at his dad. Doug Powers had never looked so bad: his hair was long, shaggy, and matted, with a grey beard growing over his face and neck;

87

clothes were ragged and torn; his bare feet grimy and callused. It was hard to believe his dad was old. He really had not seen him for almost two years, but something made him look old and tired: the way he moved, the way he felt for things.

"Well, what's your plan, Son?"

"My plan? For what?"

"The plan to get us out of here."

"I was hoping that you had a plan." said Josh sheepishly. "I really don't think we can get out. Carlos Martinez wants to get rid of us. I sorta insulted him when I said you had been kidnapped."

Doug Powers smiled. "Joshua, nothing is impossible with God. I believe God brought you safely here to deliver me from my enemies."

"I don't know how safe we are. I'm locked in here with you."

"God will deliver. There's a verse in the Bible that has guided my whole life. In fact, it's why I named you Joshua. 'Have I not commanded you? Be strong and courageous. Do not be terrified, do not be discouraged—'"

"'for the Lord your God will be with you wherever you go.' I found that verse on a small scrap of paper in my old room."

"Joshua, a man can't go wrong if he puts all of his hope in the Lord. Life's situations change things, but the love and hope that God gives, remain forever. That's all we can count on."

Josh didn't understand all of that, but he thought God had helped him the last few days, and he knew his dad had trusted God for a long time.

"So, Josh, where did you land the airplane?"

For the first time Josh was embarrassed about the crash. He had always believed that his father was the best pilot in the world, never making any mistakes.

"I ... I landed it in the river below Malo Falls." Josh' face grew warm. He turned away from his father.

"Are you all right?"

"Yeah, I'm fine. One of Martinez's men shot me down."

"Joshua, you're a good pilot. That was a tricky place to land and you pulled it off." His dad patted him on the shoulder.

"I sorta demolished the airplane. It wasn't that hot of a landing."

"Any landing you can walk away from is a good one. I'm proud of you, Son."

Josh leaned into his father and slipped his arms around the man's back. His dad returned the hug.

"I'm so glad to be with you, Dad."

Doug Powers took his son's arm and moved toward the makeshift bed. They both sat on the hard crates, the only furniture in the hangar.

"Well, Son, about your plan to escape. Tell me where we are?"

Josh turned quickly to look at his father who was staring into the greyness of the building. "Dad, don't you know where you are?"

"Not really. I know we are near a runway because I can hear my old airplane take off very early each morning and return later the same day. Now and then, I hear a jet come and go."

"How long have you been here?"

"I've been in this room since I was kidnapped. It seems like forever. They came to the compound in the middle of the night and carried me out. When I resisted, one of them hit me with something. When I came to, I was hogtied on the floor of my airplane with a gunnysack over my aching head."

"And this is the only place you've seen?"

"When I first got here, they threw me in the back of an old truck. I don't know where they took me. A man with a high voice accused me of working for the American government."

"That was Carlos Martinez." Josh interrupted.

"When I told him I was a missionary, all he said was, 'We will see.' Then they drove me here, and threw me in this building. It took me three days to work the ropes off my wrists."

"Have they told you anything else?"

"Not a word. If it wasn't for Randy, I would have starved to death a long time ago."

The mention of food brought on the hunger pains. "Dad, do you have any food? I'm starving," Josh said.

"Randy will bring dinner to us tonight. I don't keep food here. I don't want them to suspect that anyone is bringing me something to eat. Now, tell me what's outside."

"Well, we're in a metal hangar on a new paved runway. The runway is about a mile long. Across from here, is a little shack with a guard. He is probably watching us."

"Are there any airplanes kept here?"

"Your airplane is here and that business jet you heard. Dad, maybe you can fly us out in that jet."

"If we are going to fly out of here, we will take our own airplane. That way, we only take what's ours." Doug Powers sighed.

"Do you have a plan, Dad?"

"I have an idea that we'll talk over with Randy when he gets here."

For the next few hours they talked of the past and how much they both missed Josh' mother. Home seemed so far away, and it felt as if neither had been there for years.

"Dad, do you think that mom's okay?"

"Joshua, your mother is fine. She is with friends who love her and are praying for her and for us. Before you know it, we'll all be back together."

Doug Powers was interrupted by a blood curdling scream from the jungle behind the metal hangar. Josh jumped and nudged closer to his dad. After a pause, there was a short, mournful howl followed by another painful scream.

"That's Randy." Doug Powers held his forefinger over his lips. "I told you he was all right. That's just the way Randy rings the doorbell."

A few more minutes went by and Randy began to rant and rave. The mumbling went on until one of the guards across the runway, fired a burst from his machine gun. Randy let out a screech, and ran back into the jungle.

"He'll be back in a little while." Josh' dad smiled.

Josh checked his watch. He was hungry and though he wanted Randy to be safe, his hunger had all of his attention. Every few minutes Josh checked his watch. They waited thirty minutes which seemed longer than the last few days.

Josh leaned against the wall of the hangar, closed his eyes, and tried not to think about food. When he opened his eyes, he was startled to see the outline of a hairy man standing in the shadows of the room. Josh, still sitting next to his dad on the bed, jammed his elbow into Doug Powers' ribs.

"Dad, someone is in the room with us," he whispered.

"Joshua? Is that you?" Logan's hushed voice came from within the shadows. He approached quickly and knelt in front of them. "It is you."

"Ah, Randy. Glad you could make it," Doug Powers said. "Did you bring anything to eat? Joshua is real hungry."

"I've got your favorite. Roast Iguana. Are you into lizard meat, Joshua?" Logan raised his eyebrows and licked his lips.

"I'm so hungry I could eat my jacket."

"Not the way that thing smells," said Logan.

All three of them laughed quietly.

Logan handed Josh the cooked lizard meat and turned to his dad.

"Doug, I think we had better have a talk while Josh eats his dinner." Logan took Doug's arm and led him to the darker side of the room. Josh could hear their muffled voices, but was more interested in his meal.

"Dad, do you want something to eat?"

"I don't think so, Son. You finish up the meat and rest on the bed.

The two men talked for hours. Josh drifted in and out of sleep and waited for them to come back to his side of the hangar. At 2:30 in the morning the two men came and woke Josh.

"Joshua, we need to talk to you about our escape plan." Logan tugged gently on Josh' shoulder.

"What is it?" Josh rubbed the sleep from his eyes.

Doug Powers spoke softly and fast. "The first thing we need to do is get Randy's family here. He wants you to go with him and help bring them back. But you'll need to go tonight. In about an hour our old plane leaves here and you guys need to be as far away as you can."

"But Dad, what will happen to you if the guards come and I'm not here?"

"I don't think they'll come. They haven't been here in about two weeks. When they do come, they never look in. They only stand outside and shout through the wall. Besides, if they do ... well, that's a chance we just have to take."

"I don't like it, Dad."

"Joshua." Logan quietly pleaded. "I really need your help. Besides the two girls your age, we have a new baby girl. Once they're here, all of you will be able to escape."

"Let's pray so you boys can get out of here." Doug Powers bowed his head.

Before Josh could say anything else, his father started to pray. He didn't hear a word. All Josh could think about was the danger his dad would be in if the guards found out that he was not in the hangar. He wanted to argue, but he had heard the pleading tone in Logan's voice.

As soon as his father said "Amen," Josh got up.

"Well, let's get going," Josh said. He tried to be as casual as he could, but the squeak in his voice gave him away. Logan patted Doug Powers on the shoulder and walked toward the back of the hangar.

"I love you, Dad." Josh gulped. He surprised himself with that one. It was something he hadn't said for years. He started to follow Logan but then returned to his father and gave him a hug.

"I love you, Son. Thanks for coming."

Josh nodded then hurried after Logan. Randy Logan directed him to the rear of the hangar where he quietly slid a piece of metal to one side. The hole led out of the hangar behind some wooden crates Logan had stacked to hide his entrance.

They pushed the boxes back against the loose siding on the building, and crawled into the dark brush behind the hangar. Logan then made a turn and ran parallel to the runway.

Once directly across the landing strip from the jet and the Beech 18, Logan grabbed Josh' arm and pulled him to the ground. From there they crawled for fifty feet before Logan disappeared. Josh laid still and watched for any movement.

"Logan. Where are you? Logan? The glare from the lights on the parking ramp blinded Josh. Where are—" His words were cut short by a hand which clamped over his mouth. Before he could shake himself free, he was pulled into a hole.

"Joshua, you have to be quiet. The men are over by your dad's plane getting ready for the morning run to the compound. We'll wait here until they are gone," Logan whispered in his ear.

"Where is here?" Josh asked.

Logan chuckled. "I have these duck blinds all around this place. This is one of the ways I avoid the bullets. Stand up here. You can watch everything these birds do. That's why I call them duck blinds. I even have one overlooking the Palace."

Josh saw the glow of the flood lights that surrounded Carlos Martinez' world. He glanced at the airplane just in time to see the overweight pilot being hoisted in. Juan and the other gunman climbed into the plane and sat near the door, while two men in black suits stood guard.

"This drug trafficking is scary business, isn't it?" Josh clenched his fists and sighed.

"Yeah, we are a hundred miles from the nearest town and these guys all have guns, and they sleep with these giant night lights on." Logan motioned toward the glow from the flood lights.

Josh watched the old plane belch fire and smoke from its right engine. The starter whined again, and the engine roared to life. In a few seconds the left engine was running and the plane was on the move. It taxied around the jet and rolled out onto the runway.

"They're going the wrong way. Look at the windsock," Josh said.

"They're going to the hangar to gas up. This is part of their morning ritual. I figure they only put in enough gas to fly to the compound and back with a little reserve. They want to keep the weight down so they can move more drugs," Logan said. "You better try to get some sleep while we wait for them to leave."

Josh was tired and he didn't have to be told twice. He slid to the bottom of the hole and closed his eyes.

Twenty minutes later the roar of the twin engines on the Beech 18 woke Josh from a sound sleep.

Logan waited until the sound faded. "We better get going," he whispered and slithered out of the brush-trap door. Then he stuck his head back through the hole. "Stay flat on the ground when you get out here."

Josh followed Logan through the small opening into the darkness. On their bellies they crawled through the short brush along the edge of the runway. They got to their feet when they reached the trees.

"Let's go, Joshua." Logan jogged down a jungle trail.

Josh did his best to keep up. Now and then, Logan looked back to make sure Josh was still with him. If Josh got too far behind, Logan would stop and let him rest.

Josh followed Logan through the jungle for thirty minutes.

"Not much farther," Logan said. But as he rounded a sharp corner in the trail a spear pointed right at his face. "Stop! Joshua! Go back!"

Josh heard Logan's warning, but it was too late. Two Alasa warriors jumped from the brush and blocked his retreat. Logan was already surrounded by ten Alasa Indians in paint and feathers. Several more Indians emerged from the jungle and formed a tight circle around Josh.

Chapter 9

The Alasa closed in on Josh; their spears pointed at his belly. They inched toward him until the tips touched his waist.

"Yamnel! Tolando! Yamnel!" Josh shouted.

The man directly in front of him looked into his eyes. "Yamnel, Tolando?" He repeated the words then spun quickly around, and ran off into the jungle. Everyone else stood still.

A large Alasa man with a rope tied around his head, and a ring of red and blue feathers hanging from his waist, appeared out of the bush. He walked around the circle of men who surrounded Logan. His mumbling became louder as he circled. After three times around, he stared into Logan's face, then unexpectedly, blew a handful of bright yellow dust into Logan's face and onto his chest.

The stench of the yellow dust reached Josh's nostrils. He gagged. At the same time Logan started to sneeze. Every time he sneezed the Indians shouted, "Tekna"!

Then a few seconds later, Logan gagged. He threw up several times before falling to the ground and curling up into a ball.

"Logan!" Josh yelled.

But when he yelled the Alasa poked him with their spears. They didn't seem to be interested in Logan any more. One Indian remained with Logan, all the others who had been guarding Logan now stood guard over Josh. Josh stood still.

"Yamnel! Yamnel! Josh shouted again. None of the warriors moved a muscle.

Minutes passed like hours as Josh waited for what was to happen next. *Be strong and courageous for the Lord is with me.*

Logan hadn't stirred or made a noise for a half an hour. Josh was afraid he was dead. Logan's limp body lay in direct sunlight with flies buzzing around his face and head.

"Logan," Josh whispered. "Logan can you hear me?"

A faint grunt escaped from Logan's lips. Two of the warriors pointed their spears at his neck. The rest stood still with their eyes fixed on Josh.

After what seemed liked hours of painfully standing in one position, Josh was relieved when the chief, with the bright feathers, finally spoke up. All the Indians stood at attention, and raised their spears to the sky.

Josh tried to leave without drawing attention

to himself but his muscles cramped up.

The brightly dressed Alasa danced into the circle and got right into Josh' face. He grabbed the blue baseball cap off Josh' head and sniffed it. Then put the cap on his own head, only to take it take off to smell it again. "Yamnel," he said in a deep, soft voice.

"Yes." Josh looked down but reached out to rub his first three fingers down the inside of the man's forearm: the sign of friendship.

The chief's eyes widened.

"Yamnel. Tolando," Josh said again and for the second time rubbed the inside of the man's arm.

The Alasa Indian stuck the hat back on Josh' head. He said something to one of the guards who nodded, then disappeared into the jungle.

Josh sat on the ground, face to face with the Alasa chief who gently took Josh by the hand.

"Yamnel," the chief said again. It was the only word they both understood.

"Yes, Yes." Josh agreed. "Is my friend, yamnel, okay?" Josh pointed to Logan.

The chief looked at Josh, then at Logan and started to talk. He rolled his eyes wildly and danced all his fingers upon his head.

Josh pointed at Logan. "My yamnel," he said softly, patting his hand on his chest. He walked over to Logan and swiped three fingers down his forearm like he had done with the chief. "Yamnel."

The old man looked puzzled and pointed at Logan, then at Josh. "Yamnel?"

"Yes! Yes!" Josh nodded.

The old chief stood up, shrugged his shoulders, and walked into the forest. Josh was a little confused. It took ten minutes before the old man returned and sat in the dirt next to Logan's motionless body. After a long stare, he shrugged his shoulders again.

"Yamnel Hoha!"

Joshua recognized the voice coming from behind the trees. "Yamnel Tolando! Where are you?" Josh called out.

A boy much smaller than Josh walked out of the trees' shadows. He was dressed in the same bright feathers as the chief. And there was a white stripe of paint that ran from the top of his forehead to the tip of his nose.

The boy gazed up at Josh, took the blue hat off Josh' head and sniffed it just like the chief had done. Then returned it to the top of Josh's light brown hair. Both boys reached out and ran their fingers down each other's arms.

"Yamnel," they said at the same time.

Tolando saw Logan and made strange sounds, rolled his eyes, and danced his fingers on his head.

"Yamnel?" Tolando pointed at Logan.

"Yes. Yes. Logan is my friend," Josh said.

"Lu-goon friend," Tolando struggled with his words.

Josh was sure now that they wouldn't hurt Logan. "Is Logan, okay?" he asked.

"Lu-goon okay!" said Tolando. He smiled and let out a sigh of relief.

"Lu-goon okay." Logan's voice was hushed and raspy. He remained on the ground. "Amigo."

"Si, Amigo!" repeated Tolando.

"Habla espanol?" asked Logan.

"Si, si," Tolando answered.

Logan sat up and caressed his throbbing head. "Josh, he speaks Spanish. Praise God."

Josh had learned a little bit of Spanish as a child of a missionary, but Logan was fluent.

Tolando spoke to one of the warriors who then cautiously, approached Logan with his spear aimed at his throat. The warrior pulled something from a small, leather pouch hanging around his neck and handed it to Logan. Then he quickly returned to find his place back in the circle.

Tolando's Spanish was broken and filled with words from his own language. But Josh understood enough to know Tolando wanted Logan to eat the hard, brown chunk the warrior had placed in his hand.

Logan inhaled and wrinkled his nose. "He wants me to eat this thing. He says it will help my head."

"Logan, Tolando has never lied to me. It will probably work."

Logan looked at Tolando. "It's the 'probably work' that has me worried."

"Comer!" commanded Tolando.

Reluctantly, Logan stuck the brown chunk in his mouth. From the sour face he made, Josh assumed it tasted as bad as it smelled. Logan chewed and swallowed as fast as he could. The Indians smiled and mumbled amongst themselves.

Logan stiffened as if the food had turned him into a statue. "Joshua. My head stopped hurting," he said after a few minutes of silence.

"What was it?" asked Josh.

"I think it was some kind of root or something. It tasted like garlic, ginger and an onion, but it felt like a raw potato."

Logan got to his feet and spoke to Tolando in Spanish. They spoke faster than Josh could understand so he gave up and went to sit down by a tree, and closed his eyes.

When he opened his eyes he was startled by a tight little circle of warriors staring at him. Josh felt someone touch his arm. Tolando said something to the warriors who then walked in a line and disappeared into the jungle.

"Joshua, great news. The Alasa are going to help with our escape plan. They're going to help get my family to the plane. They don't like the drug dealers either. Who could blame them. They're always shooting at them. They do nothing but burn down the forest so they can grow coca for cocaine."

"When do we leave?" Josh got up and straightened out his tattered clothes.

"When the men get back. Tolando sent them to get more—"

"Hoha, Lu-goon come!"

Josh and Logan walked toward Tolando who was followed by as many as fifty Alasa warriors armed with bows, arrows, and blowguns. Tolando gave a hand signal and all of them returned to the jungle and headed for the cave where Logan's family was hiding.

"Joshua, these people are really something. They seem to know everything about the jungle. I didn't tell them where my family was, but they seem to know."

Josh nodded and smiled.

For an hour Josh and Logan followed the Indians through the jungle until they reached the cave. The opening, covered by broken branches, was just large enough for a man to crawl through. Logan led the way; Josh followed close behind. The cave was dark and damp and no one seemed to be inside.

"Honey, I'm home," Logan said with a sing-song tone. "Deb, are you here?"

"Randy?" Debbie Logan's voice echoed from behind a pile of rocks in the back of the cave. She came out running and threw her arms around his neck. "I'm so glad you're back. They found us."

"Who found you?" Randy asked.

"Some of Martinez's men. One of them came in and threatened us. When he went outside to get help, I heard a struggle and then it was silent. No one came back to get us."

"Deb, I have a surprise for you. Joshua Powers is here. He's come to get you out."

Debbie turned to Josh and hugged him. "I'm so glad to see you. Did you bring an airplane big enough to carry all of us?"

"Well, I—" Josh was interrupted by movement in the back of the cave.

"Joshua, you remember Ashley?" Randy pointed to a girl about Josh' age.

"Yes ... Yes, I do. Hi," Josh stammered. He could feel his face grow warm. Ashley was the prettiest girl he had ever seen, even with a dirt-smudged face and uncombed hair. He had a hard time not looking at her, and every time he glanced, he caught her looking at him. In his embarrassment he kept his eyes on the ground.

"And this is Amy," Debbie Logan said.

Josh went through the whole red-faced routine again. Amy was only a year younger then Ashley and just as pretty.

"Where's the baby?" asked Logan.

"Randy, the baby is sick. She has a high fever and coughs all the time. She might have croup or something."

"That's probably how Martinez's men found you. I think we better get out of here as fast as we can," Josh said.

"The baby is too sick to travel. I think we better ..." Debbie Logan suddenly screamed and pushed the girls behind Randy. Josh and Logan spun around ready to face the looming danger.

Then Josh blew out a sigh of relief. "Tolando, you took ten years off my life!"

Tolando had slipped through the small opening into the cave and was standing in the shadows.

"This is my friend Tolando, yamnel Tolando," said Josh.

Logan introduced Tolando to his family. The young Alasa touched the girls' blonde hair and softly spoke to them in his Spanish-Indian mix.

Logan chuckled. "These Indians don't see many blonde-headed people out here in the jungle, do they?"

Tolando began to speak louder and faster than Josh had ever heard. He waved his arms, gesturing toward the door. Logan listened carefully and asked questions as he tried to understand what Tolanda was saying. With all the commotion and loud talking the sleeping baby awoke. She screamed and began to cough.

Debbie Logan ran to their hiding place behind the rocks and brought out another blonde baby girl. Tolando moved forward and stroked the baby's head, but then turned to Logan and started gibbering again. After a few seconds, Tolando turned and slithered out of the small cave entrance.

"Tolando says we must leave as soon as we can" Randy started gathering his family together.

"But Randy, the baby—"

"Four armed men are headed this way. Tolando's warrior spotted them about a quarter of a mile from here. We don't have much time. Don't take anything with you."

The Logan girls both ran behind the rock and returned with crudely made grass sandals. Ashley slipped a small Bible into the pocket of her dress while Mrs. Logan wrapped the baby in a blanket and tried to comfort her.

"Well, that about does it," Josh said. "Last one out turn off the lights and lock the door."

Everyone laughed.

Josh was the first to exit out of the small opening and waited for the others to crawl out. Each one of them shaded their eyes with their hands and squinted in the bright sunlight.

"Let's pray before we go. Joshua you pray for us," said Logan.

Before Josh could protest, everyone closed their eyes. Josh stood speechless. He couldn't remember the last time he prayed in front of anyone. Maybe he never had. At the very least, he knew he was out of practice. The silence made him uneasy.

"Dear God." There was a long painful pause. "Dear God," Josh said again. All he could think of was the verse he had found on that tiny scrap of paper.

"Dear God, you said that we should be brave and strong because you are with us. Be with us today. Amen. Ah, In Jesus' name, Amen."

In the meantime, Tolando had crept up to the little circle and pushed his head into the middle.

"Yamnel Hoha, Lu-goon, Go!"

"It's time to go," Josh said.

With Tolando leading the way, Josh and the Logan family made their escape through the jungle at a very fast pace. It wasn't long before the girls fell behind. Josh held back to help them. Every time Ashley looked at him, he felt his face flush.

Amy was following a few steps behind Josh and Ashley. When they crossed a small stream, she slipped on a wet, green, moss-covered stone and fell face down in the water. Her scream sent the birds into a frenzy. Josh quickly helped Amy out of the water.

"Are you alright? he whispered.

"It hurts." Amy began to wail.

Tolando came back and stared at the girl. He said something softly in his Indian dialect. Nobody knew what it was, but they could tell it was an order.

The line of people continued their journey through the forest. A warrior appeared out of the tree cover and whispered to Tolando who turned to the group and made a hand motion. Josh recognized the gesture. It was the silence signal Tolando had taught him. Josh turned to the Logan family and put his index finger across his lips.

But the silence was broken by the cry and coughing of the baby. As the baby's cough grew louder, voices could be heard in the distance. The gunmen were moving in on the sound.

Tolando whispered something to one of the warriors who nodded then ran into the jungle.

Tolando spun around and motioned for another warrior. The warrior's hand went up his own throat and he ran his finger across his neck.

"Don't kill them!" Logan said. He grabbed Tolando's arm and repeated it again in Spanish. Tolando frowned at Logan and then at Josh.

"Don't kill them." Josh repeated.

Tolando seemed puzzled and shrugged his shoulders. He then turned to another warrior and whispered in his ear. This warrior also vanished into the gray darkness of the tree line.

Moments later the first warrior returned with a handful of green leaves. Taking the leaves, Tolando went back to the baby and placed two leaves inside his own mouth and chewed. He pulled the wad out of his mouth and tried to put it in the baby's mouth.

"What are you doing?" Debbie Logan snapped.

"It's okay." Logan crawled next to his wife. "Tolando can be trusted. He gave me something that cured the pain in my head."

Tolando held out his hand to Mrs. Logan and gesture for her to put some in her own mouth.

"No." Her voice quivered as she looked at her husband.

Logan took the leaves from Tolando and stuffed them into his mouth. "It tastes like peppermint." He took the baby into his arms and removed the small wad of chewed leaves.

Debbie Logan trembled. She seemed unsure and frightened as she wiped a tear from her face. But she helped her husband open the baby's mouth. The baby moved the green goo around for few seconds and stopped coughing.

But loud angry voices were coming up behind them; close enough to understand each word. Then, suddenly, the gunmen's shouts of anger and bravado turned into screams of terror.

Tolando turned to the group and smiled. "Let's go." He stood up and calmly walked into the jungle. Everyone scrambled to their feet and followed.

Chapter 10

Josh crawled on his scraped hands and bruised knees to the edge of the forest. There were still two hours of daylight left and Logan told him to go back into the metal hangar. There were guards everywhere. The two guards across the runway from the hangar were playing catch with a seed pod from one of the trees. Several men unloaded the drugs from his dad's Beech 18.

Josh lay glaring at the outside walls of the metal building. He really wanted to wait until dark, but Logan thought it would leave his father in danger with so many people around. And Logan didn't want to do his crazy American screaming act with his family so close; a stray bullet could injure or kill one of them.

Stalling as long as he could, Josh decided it was time to go. There was about twenty-five feet of open ground to cover. Josh shifted to his left hoping the hangar would hide him from the guards' view, and that the men unloading the plane were too busy to notice. Taking three deep breaths, he slithered across the bare ground toward the building.

"Hey! Hey! What are you doing?" an angry voice shouted.

Josh pressed his body into the ground and waited for the roar of gunfire. It never came. He raised his ear to the wind but he couldn't hear anyone running toward him. The guards were still laughing and playing catch. Slowly, he lifted his head to see his father's airplane. He took a count of all the men; each seemed to be accounted for and unloading the cargo. With a sigh of relief, Josh crawled toward the hangar. Five feet from the wall he heard a mean voice shouting.

"Old man! We have some food for you and your kid."

Josh hugged the earth. There was no response from his father.

"Old man, get up! Come to the door." A guard pounded on the front of the building with his fist.

"I can't come to the door, just leave the food inside and we'll get it," Doug Powers replied in a soft voice.

"Send that boy to the door!"

"He can't come right now."

Josh heard the man fumbling with the keys for the lock on the metal door. In matter of seconds his father could get hurt. Without further thought, Josh bolted to the boxes that covered the secret entrance. Moving the boxes as quietly as he could, he slid through the hole in the back of the hangar. Then pulled the loose metal back into place just as the guard opened the door. A shaft of light split the room in half.

Grabbing a piece of wood from the floor, Josh flung it against the wall. He hoped the guard would think that was the sound heard when Josh was pushing the boxes out of the way.

"Can't a guy have any privacy." Josh grumbled as loud as he could as he walked to the door.

"Quiet! Take this food before I feed it to the rats," the guard growled. "Mr. Martinez says to enjoy it because you won't need any breakfast."

Josh took the plate of food from the man's hand. When the door slammed behind him, he ran to his father on the bed.

"Thank the Lord. You're back," Doug Powers whispered. "Talk about timing."

"Yeah, that was close." Josh picked up a half-eaten chicken from his plate. "Dad, we're getting out of here tonight. When it's dark and the guards have settled down, we'll make a break for it."

"Is Randy ready to go?"

"Yeah. His family is hidden about a hundred yards from here." Josh tore a leg off the chicken and handed it to his dad.

"Thank you Father for this food," Doug Powers prayed.

Josh bowed his head, a little embarrassed that he hadn't thought of praying for their meal.

"Amen."

"Dad, they unloaded our plane. I hope it has gas."

"Joshua, God will take care of our needs if we trust him."

Josh took one bite of meat. "I'm going to take a nap and get ready for tonight." He lay down on the ground near his father's bed.

But Josh didn't rest at all. He turned from side to side trying to get comfortable. Sleep was interrupted by haunting night sounds and annoying body aches. Every time he woke he checked his watch. Time dragged on. Fear of failure kept his mind racing. Josh was glad his dad and Logan were there to fly them all to safety.

Doug Powers' firm, rough hand rubbed the back of Josh's neck. "Come on, Son. It's time to go."

Josh rolled over and rubbed his eyes.

"Joshua, there's a major get-together up at the Palace which leaves only one guard left across the runway," said Logan. "The Alasa will keep him busy."

"What's the plan?" Josh tried to sound braver than he felt.

"You and I will lead Randy's family to the plane," Doug Powers said.

"Let's get going. Your dad can fill in the details on the way." Logan walked toward the loose metal at the rear of the hangar.

"Protect us, Lord." Doug Powers put his hand on Josh' shoulder. "Lead the way, Son."

That familiar touch of his father's hand, made Josh feel safe. His dad always seemed to know just what he needed.

Maneuvering through the dark, musty room toward their secret opening gave Josh a sense of freedom. He couldn't wait to get on that airplane and fly away from
these criminals.

Logan squeezed through the slot in the wall. "Watch your head, Doug."

Josh slipped through the hole next and waited for his father. Doug Powers took a few steps and stumbled over the trash. Josh lounged forward and caught him by the arm.

"You better keep your hand on my shoulder, Dad, until we get to the tree line," Josh said with a little bit of authority.

His dad stood up straight and took several deep breaths. "Oh. This fresh air smells so good. I almost forgot how I love the smell of the jungle."

Josh pulled him gently to the ground. "Dad, we need to be quiet," he whispered under his breath. "Hold onto my shirt, we're going to go to the tree line." *Father, thank you for my dad. Help me to know you, like he does.*"

"Joshua ... over here."

Josh turned and led his father toward a muffled voice coming just to their right.

"Doug Powers, it's really good to see you." It was Debbie Logan who greeted them.

"Debbie? It's good to hear your voice," Doug Powers replied.

"I hate to cut this short, but we need to get moving," Logan interrupted. "Joshua, lead your dad and my family to the plane. Stay well back in the trees. Just keep your eyes on the light over the planes.

"We have to be quiet." Josh reminded everyone. "You girls stay right behind me. Mrs. Logan you and the baby next and Dad, you bring up the rear."

Doug Powers dad placed his hand on Debbie Logan's shoulder.

Josh took Ashley Logan's hand and quietly led everyone through the bush. When he realized he was holding Ashley's hand, he blushed. He tried to let go, but Ashley held on.

Suddenly, a blood curdling scream ripped the night air and Josh dropped to one knee. "Down everyone. Get down." He crawled along the line of people. "Stay here and don't make a sound."

On his belly, Josh continued to the edge of the trees. In the dim light of the guard shack, Josh could see the ghostly figures of the Alasa attacking the guard, then carried him off into the darkness. Josh waited a few minutes to make sure no alarm was sent to the Palace. When it was safe, he crawled back to the group.

"The Alasa took the guard, but we still need to be quiet. He may have warned his friends. Let's go."

As soon as Josh came back Ashley took his hand. They were all tired but plodded forward. When they reached the runway and spotted the airplane, Josh' heart raced with nerves and adrenaline.

It had been easy to move in the darkness of the tree line, but now they had to cross the open space of the runway. The bright flood lights over the planes lit up the runway as if it was day.

"I think you better wait here while I check it out," Josh whispered as he crouched low to the ground.

"You be careful, Son."

Josh took a glimpse over his shoulder and smiled at his dad. "Father, make me strong and courageous. Lord be with me." Josh prayed silently.

Then he stepped out of the safety of the tree line and into the bright light. The light color of his clothing against the background of the dark jungle, stood out like a black fly in a bowl of white rice.

A few steps onto the runway, Josh heard the roar and squeaks of the old army truck. He spun and dove for the edge of the blacktop. Through one eye, he saw the bouncing lights of the approaching vehicle. The old truck stopped between Josh and he airplane.

A man, well-dressed and armed, jumped out of the truck and studied the bags of cocaine piled under the wings of the jet. The driver used a powerful spotlight to inspect both planes and the surrounding area.

The gunman returned to the truck and threw his weapon onto the seat. Taking the spotlight from the driver, he hopped onto the hood of the truck and shined the light directly at Josh.

"Edwardo! Where are you? Edwardo!" He yelled several times for the guard.

Josh' heart beat began to beat faster. He tried not to move a muscle as the light was kept right on him. Josh wondered if he should stand and surrender to keep these men from finding the others. His whole body tingled with fear and sweat ran down his face. All of a sudden, the light shot up into the air above him.

Dropping the light, the man dove back into the truck, legs dangling over the door, as the driver slammed his foot down on the gas pedal. The truck careened around the back of the airplanes and headed up the road toward the Palace. Josh turned his head enough to see the thirty Alasa warriors slipping back into the jungle.

Josh sprang into action and ran to his friends who were huddled in a tight circle, praying.

"Thank you Lord," Debbie Logan whispered.

Josh plopped on the ground next to them.

"Maybe we should go around the end of the runway," she said. "We would be in too much danger crossing the strip right under the lights."

"I think that would take too long. Those guys might have seen me. The Alasa scared them off, for now." Josh said. "But we need to get out of here as fast as we can. I'm going to cross and see if I can find a hiding place."

Doug Powers tried to stop his son, but Josh acted like he didn't hear him.

Josh darted to the edge of the trees and hid just outside the light. He really didn't want to cross the blacktop, but before he could change his mind, he ran as fast as he could.

The blacktop was the longest one hundred feet Josh had ever run. His eyes kept scanning for any suspicion activity and searched the area for a place to hide. The only place that looked safe was the jumbled pile of drugs. He headed for the burlap bags.

Diving onto the bags, Josh slithered to the dark side of the pile and sat very still. He tried to listen, but he couldn't hear anything over his breathing. When he was satisfied that no one was around, he slowly lifted his head above the bags looking for a place his dad and the Logan family could hide.

The two airplanes were sitting in the middle of the light-bathed ramp. The jet facing the runway and his dad's airplane faced the opposite direction. He would have to hide everyone in his dad's plane. It was the only safe place.

Josh got into a track runner's crouch. He sprang to running position and dashed across the runway. The bright light at his back made it hard for him to see as he sprinted into the darkness. But when he reached the edge of the pavement, he stumbled and fell. The pain of skinned hands and knees shot through his body as he tumbled along the ground from his stomach to his back.

The accident gave him a chance to catch his breath, so he laid there for as long as he could.

Before he could get to his feet, a hand grabbed his arm and pulled him to his feet. Two Alasa warriors came to his rescue and walked him safely back to the rest of the group. The older warrior brushed the dirt and sticks from Josh' dirty hair and face.

"What do you think, Joshua?" asked Logan.

"The only place to hide is in the airplane. I think it will be safe," Josh replied.

"Well, we're not going to wait too long. Once we get into the plane we'll need to put the next part of our plan into action. Logan hugged his daughters. "Besides, the Alasa have a little surprise for these guys."

Chapter 11

"Joshua, take your dad over to the plane and start going through the pre-flight check list. When I get my family there, I'll pre-flight the outside." Logan hurried through his instructions.

Let's go Dad." Josh was so eager to leave that he had stopped thinking about the danger.

Doug Powers got up slowly, his hands out in front of him, but he stumbled over someone's feet. Logan caught him and kept him from falling.

Josh reached out to his father and took him by the arm. He was worried about his dad. Josh frowned. *He must be sicker than he lets on.* Doug Powers was usually "a take charge" kind of person.

"Are you ready?" Josh loosened his grip on his father's arm.

"Lead the way, Son." Doug Powers' hand fumbled for the back of Josh' shirt and took a handful of its ragged material.

"Don't try to run, Joshua" said Logan. "The Alasa are all around us here. They'll be our eyes and ears."

At the edge of the tree line Josh peered around the area they had to cross. "All clear," he said. "Well, let's go." Josh pulled his father into the light and as quietly as possible, they walked across the runway.

The short journey seemed like it took forever. Josh' eyes narrowed, his ears on alert for any sign of danger. When they reached the middle of the runway a loud crash came from the hangar where they had been imprisoned.

"Down! Get down!" Josh fell to the ground.

Both he and his father laid flat and still.

Josh twisted his body to view the hangar. In the dark, he could barely make out its shape. With no guard in the shack across the runway, Josh was satisfied that there was no threat and got to his feet.

"Let's go, Dad. I think it's safe." He helped his father up. This time he waited for his dad to get a grip on the back of his shirt. They both moved a little faster.

Reaching the airplane, Josh hid in the shadow of the wing and pulled his father down to the ground.

"Bet you're glad to see this old thing."

"How does it look?" asked his dad.

"It looks really bad, but it still flies."

"That's all we need for now."

Josh left his father on the ground and checked the open cargo door on the side of the plane. Cautiously, he stuck his head through the door and looked inside. There were still three bags of drugs on the floor of the plane. The inside smelled of the trees they mulched on his flight to the Palace.

Pulling himself into the plane, he pushed one of the bags out the door and then did the same with the other two. Josh piled the bags next to the plane to make stairs.

"Pssst. Pssst. Dad, let's get going."

When Doug Powers stood up he bumped his head on the underside of the wing. He took a deep breath and gathered himself. Then with his right hand he traced the edge of the wing. From there, as he moved down the side of the plane he tripped over the bags that Josh had piled up.

Josh leapt out of the plane and landed right by his side "Dad, are you okay?"

"Yeah, fine. Joshua I don't see very well these days."

"Very well? What does that mean? You can see, can't you?

"All I see is shadows. In this light, I can barely make out the shape of the plane."

"Why didn't you tell me?

"I thought you could tell by the way I stumbled and tripped over everything."

Josh didn't know what else to say as he brought his father through the door of the plane. They made their way into the cockpit. Doug Powers sat in the co-pilot's seat and Josh slid himself into the left one.

"Turn on the master switch and see how much gas this baby has in it," Doug Powers said.

Josh located the switch on the panel. He flipped it to the on position. The familiar whirs and whines began as some of the instruments came to life.

"Looks like we have about a quarter tank in each wing."

"Where are we exactly?" asked his dad.

"We're fifteen or twenty miles due east of our old compound."

"We should have enough gas to get us to El Malino. It's only about sixty miles northwest of here. We won't have much reserve, but we'll make it." Doug Powers leaned back in his seat, closed his eyes, and ran through the check list from memory.

When he called out an item, Josh's hands would respond. Halfway through the check list, Josh felt the plane move. His hand shot across the aisle and gently placed his fingers on his father lips. Someone climbed through the rear door. Josh froze. His hands balled into fists. He waited.

"You boys about ready to go?" Logan's voice was soft and steady.

Josh and his father let out a sigh at the same time.

"Did we scare ya?" Logan was trying to keep his laughter down to a whisper.

"Logan, take over as pilot. I'll help everyone get settled." Josh started to get out of his seat.

125

"Keep your seat, Joshua. I'm not going."

"You have to go! Dad can't see. He can't fly the plane."

"No. But you can," Logan said.

"Me! I have never flown this the Beech 18 before."

"Joshua, you have flown this airplane hundreds of times." His dad gently reminded him.

"Dad, you were always on the controls. You were always there to correct my mistakes. How can you do that if you can't see? I can't do this."

"You have to." Logan interrupted the conversation.

"Why can't *you* go?" Josh shot back.

"I contacted the DEA. They're going to make a raid in a little while. Besides, I can create a diversion for you. You can do it, Joshua."

Josh slumped back into the pilot's seat. "If you say so," he muttered. He really had no confidence in himself right now.

"Let's finish the check list. It's like going out for a Sunday tour," Doug Powers said. "Now, where were we?"

Josh could hear Logan getting his family seated and secured. The baby woke and the muffled cries distracted him.

Logan stuck his head into the cockpit and smiled that crazy smile. "Captain Powers, your passengers are

126

all loaded and their seat belts are fastened. Should I serve lunch now?"

"Yes, that would be fine." Josh tried to sound funny, but his voice was shaky.

"We're done with the check list," his dad said.

"Good. Joshua when you start these engines I don't know what the bad guys will do," Logan said. "When you get one engine started, rev it up, turn the airplane toward the runway, and begin taxiing. Start the other engine on the run. It might get a little scary, so prime both engines before you start."

"How much longer should I wait." Josh stirred in his seat and wiped the sweat from his forehead.

"Just a few more minutes. The Alasa will dump fuel on the drug pile around the other airplane. When I slap the side of the plane, flip the switch and get moving."

Logan prepared to exit the plane.

"Randy, you be careful," Doug Powers said. "I know you want to get these guys, but don't take any chances."

"Chances? Not me." Logan smiled. "See you in El Molino."

Josh reached up and threw both switches for the booster pumps and primed the engines. He tried not to think about what he had to do. The lives of all these people were in his hands. His mouth was dry and his heart was beating a hole in his chest. Before he could worry himself much more, he heard Logan slap the side of the plane.

"Father, give me strength and courage for this trip. Help me remember all I am supposed to do. Protect these passengers." Josh had no problem praying out loud.

"Amen!" Doug Powers beamed with pride. "Okay Son, start the left engine first."

Moving his hand to the switch, Josh hesitated but then flipped the lever to start the engine. He steadied his hands and switched on the starter. The familiar whine was a comfort as he remembered how to fly the plane. The engines turned over several times, caught and roared to life as Josh advanced the throttle.

His father leaned over as close as he could. "Give it some power and release the parking brake. When it starts to move it will want to turn left. You'll need to turn the plane slowly to the right until it is facing the runway."

Josh nodded as he pushed the throttle forward. The Beech 18 shook as it strained against the brakes. Josh reached down between the seats and released the brake. The plane began to move across the ground.

Just as his father had said, the plane wanted to turn to the left. His foot slammed down on the right pedal, but the plane kept turning. It was headed for the jet parked nearby.

"Dad! I can't stop it from going left. We're goin' to hit the jet." But Josh' panic was interrupted as he felt

128

the right pedal push farther down and straighten out the path of the plane.

"Get going on the other engine," his dad shouted over the roar.

Josh reached up and flipped the second switch. The starter whined; the engine turned over. There was loud backfire as a bright flame flashed from the exhaust pipe. After a second backfire, the engine roared to life.

Josh turned the airplane onto the runway. Through the side window, he saw the Alasa torch the aviation fuel that covered the bags of drugs.

But then, two cars careened out of the darkness and raced toward the plane. Josh pushed both throttles forward to full power as fast as he could without stalling the engines. With both engines running wide open, the plane started pulling to the left. He pushed down on the right pedal to get it back to the center of the runway.

"Dad! I can't keep it going straight!

"Use the trim," shouted his father.

Josh reached for the trim wheel, and a couple of turns took the pressure off his foot.

One of the cars pulled up parallel to the plane. Two men leaned out the windows and pointed their guns.

Josh was still having a hard time keeping the plane straight. His weaving from one side of the runway to the other, made the car's driver swerve as well. One of the men fired his gun. Three or four bullets struck the nose of the plane with the same sound that Josh had heard before his crash.

The plane swerved again; the driver of the car careened off the runway, crashing into the soft dirt and rolling the car over on its top.

Josh looked for the other car, but couldn't find it. He pushed forward on the control wheel and slowly lifted the tail of the plane off the ground. With the tail up, the plane gained speed. Josh gently pulled back on the wheel.

A huge bright flash caught his attention. The metal hangar which had been their prison, erupted like a volcano. Barrels of flaming aviation fuel flew through the air like bottle rockets. The shockwave from the explosion caused the airplane to shudder.

"What was that?" Doug Powers shouted.

"The hangar blew up," Josh replied.

In the light of the flames, Josh saw that the old army truck was parked in the middle of the runway.

"Dad! Grab the wheel. Help me pull it off the ground."

"It doesn't sound like it's ready to fly, Joshua," his dad said.

"There's a truck on the runway!" Josh and his dad pulled back on the wheel. The old plane shook as it lifted off the ground. Josh' hand flashed to the landing gear lever and moved it to the up position.

"You're not putting the landing gear up are you?" snapped his father.

"We won't clear the truck if I don't."

The landing gear thumped into place and both green lights came on.

"Don't climb too fast," Doug Powers said. "Hold it in level flight to build up some speed."

As they approached the truck the men ran for their lives. Tiny bursts of light from the muzzles of the guns scattered everywhere. Josh could hear the occasional slap as a bullet struck the plane.

"Is everyone alright?" Josh shouted into the back of the plane.

A few seconds later Ashley stuck her head into the cockpit.

"Is everyone okay?" Josh asked again.

"Everyone is fine," Ashley said as she patted his shoulder.

"Okay then." Josh checked his instruments to see if he had oil pressure. Then he checked the engine temperature. Both engines, on full power, were running hot. The airplane raced along only twenty feet off the ground.

Another explosion from the ground rocked the plane. Everyone in the back screamed.

"What was that?" Doug Powers asked.

"The jet blew up." Josh leaned back in his seat. "Hold on." He pulled the airplane into a steep climb. As he cleared the trees, he leveled off and drew gently back on the throttles.

The plane climbed slowly into the night sky. Glancing back at the runway, Josh saw the business jet engulfed in flames. "I think we made it," he said.

"I just hope we have enough gas to get to the city," Doug Powers replied.

Suddenly, a bright light from a helicopter illuminated the whole plane, inside and out.

"This is the Drug Enforcement Agency! We will follow you to El Molino!"

Josh waved his hand not knowing if they could see him or not. The bright light went off as the Logan family clapped and cheered.

Soon the sky was cluttered with six more helicopters as they swooped in on the airport; their lights like fingers pointing down at the runway. Josh could see even more helicopters hovering around the Palace. The DEA was after Carlos Martinez. Josh wished he could have witnessed Martinez' capture but he set his sight on EL Molino, sixty miles away.

Twenty minutes later he picked up the radio. "Mayday! Mayday! Mayday! El Molino, this is 4-6 Romeo, over."

"4-6 Romeo. What is your emergency?"

"El Molino, we have six souls on board rescued from drug dealers, including three women, a baby and one injured man. Requesting medical attention and landing instructions, over."

"4-6 Romeo. Use runway 26. All traffic is clear."

132

Josh cut the power and skillfully maneuvered for final approach. His spirit lifted. Even the airplane seemed to float gently down to earth. It touched ground with only one small bounce. And as he crossed the end of the runway, up near the terminal, Josh spotted his mother standing in the light. He smiled.

"Thank you, Father," Josh prayed out loud, "for bringing us to safety."

And everyone shouted, "Amen!"

Made in the USA
San Bernardino, CA
08 March 2020